Second Coming 2012

The Mayan Revelation

T0302795

First published by O Books, 2010
O Books is an imprint of John Hunt Publishing Ltd., The Bothy, Deershot Lodge, Park Lane, Ropley,
Hants, SO24 0BE, UK
office1@o-books.net
www.o-books.net

Distribution in:

UK and Europe
Orca Book Services
orders@orcabookservices.co.uk
Tel: 01202 665432 Fax: 01202 666219
Int. code (44)

USA and Canada
NBN
custserv@nbnbooks.com
Tel: 1 800 462 6420 Fax: 1 800 338 4550

Australia and New Zealand
Brumby Books
sales@brumbybooks.com.au
Tel: 61 3 9761 5535 Fax: 61 3 9761 7095

Far East (offices in Singapore, Thailand,
Hong Kong, Taiwan)
Pansing Distribution Pte Ltd
kemal@pansing.com
Tel: 65 6319 9939 Fax: 65 6462 5761

South Africa
Stephan Phillips (pty) Ltd
Email: orders@stephanphillips.com
Tel: 27 21 4489839 Telefax: 27 21 4479879

Text copyright Nevill Drury 2009

Design: Tom Davies

ISBN: 978 1 84694 334 8

A CIP catalogue record for this book is available
from the British Library.

Printed by Digital Book Print

Second Coming 2012

The Mayan Revelation

Nevill Drury

BOOKS

Winchester, UK
Washington, USA

By the same author:

The Shaman's Quest

'This poetic, useful and worthwhile work could become a classic.'
Publisher's Weekly, New York

'*The Shaman's Quest* speaks to me of dreams, longings and the call of ancient wisdoms, for the re-enchantment of the world and healing of the bewildered human heart.'
Ann Faraday, author of *Dream Power and The Dream Game*

'Every person has a place within the wellspring of their being that is sacred and holy. *The Shaman's Quest* ignites a potent awakening of these inner, ancient and mystical spaces
… and life is much the richer for it.'
Denise Linn, author of *Sacred Space*

Note to readers:

The events described in this book take place just prior to the appointment of Cardinal Joseph Ratzinger as Pope Benedict XVI.

�’∾ᴄ

Part One

Xocomil

�’∾ᴄ

1

AS HE LOOKED OUT across the vast shimmering lake, the old man knew he would soon depart this world. Now in his final days they were caring for him as well as they could. They had made a simple bed for him in a sheltered area adjoining the family's thatched stone and stucco hut. It was a special vantage point within the family compound where he could look out during the day at the lake and surrounding mountains.

Nachancan knew he would soon be journeying through the night sky, out along the pathway that led through the stars to Xibalba, the realm of the departed ones. There he would dwell in peace beneath the welcoming shade tree his people knew as Yaxche, a tree broader and taller than the entire world. Only then would he be reunited with the gods and ancestors of his people, the ancient ones who had helped shape and enrich his life.

He was a proud and dignified man, much loved by his family, and greatly respected by members of the other Mayan communities scattered around the lake. The other shamans were in awe of him too. Not so much because of the formidable power of his magic, which was unquestioned, but because his vision was far-reaching, the depth of his wisdom unsurpassed. While some village shamans sought power only for themselves and called on the gods and spirit-helpers to serve their own wilful desires at the expense of others, it had fallen to Nachancan to fulfil a very different role.

Nachancan was the custodian of the sacred Calendar Wheel, the shaman charged with opening the path of the Sacred Way. His people knew that when he performed his ceremonial duties the ancient ones were nourished, the crops prospered, the needs of families were met, and the path of the seasons moved forward to the final time.... the day when, as they all knew, the world would change forever.

Now, as Nachancan looked out at the vast blue lake and the three densely -wooded volcanoes that graced its shores, he knew that the ancient ones were calling him, that the time of his final journey was near.

Pulling his thick red and purple blanket up close around his shoulders to stay warm, he reflected on the many long years he had shared with his loyal and loving wife Zafrina. How she had spent hour after hour at her loom, tirelessly weaving the fabrics that would clothe the entire family. How she ungrudgingly laboured in their scattered hillside plots, tending to the crops of corn, chillis, quiscil squash and tomatoes. How she went down each day to the village marketplace and sat on her blanket on the large grey paving stones to sell whatever extra produce she had mustered. And how she would make hot corn tortillas each day, wrapping them in small offcuts of cloth, so the children had something to feed their seemingly bottomless bellies...

Together they had raised a fine family, a family to be proud of, but it was also a family beset by tragedy like so many other families around the lake. His parents and his two oldest sons, all of whom had lived with him until this terrible time, had been brutally murdered during the civil war as havoc and wanton destruction swept through the entire country. Then, soon afterwards, Zafrina's mother and sister had been swept away in a landslide following the earthquakes that devastated the country, taking thousands of lives and leaving a million people homeless. But those tragic events had taken place many seasons ago. Now a new feeling of hope was beginning to return, both to the land and to the people themselves.

Today, despite his failing eyesight, Nachancan could see that many fishermen were out sailing their dugout canoes on Lake Atitlán, casting their nets and testing their long spears against the wiles of the darting fish. Other men would be out climbing in the mountains around the lake, cutting wood and then bringing it home in bundles balanced skilfully on their backs. And the women would have their vegetables, fruit and cut flowers trussed up in their headbands of colourful cloth, with the children trailing along behind them.

But Nachancan knew that an urgent matter was now at hand. In the few remaining days ahead he would have to name his successor, name the new custodian of the sacred Calendar Wheel – the one assigned to open the path of the Sacred Way. A choice would have to be made between his two remaining sons, Itzamna and the younger one, Arana. And the choice itself was a hard one to make. Nachancan knew it would bring pride and honour to his nominated successor as well as deep hurt to the one overlooked for this important task. Nevertheless, he felt a sense of profound reassurance in the certain knowledge that his daughter Malinali would willingly support either of her two brothers. And he knew she would support Zafrina by helping with the sacred women's ceremonies and seeking guidance from the Lake Mother by reading the omens that were signals from the future.

Late that afternoon, as the setting sun sent little flecks of golden light darting across the shimmering lake, Nachancan called his two sons, Itzamna and Arana, to his bedside. They knew immediately why they had been summoned. They both felt a deep and lingering sadness in their hearts, knowing full well that the final parting was not far away.

'Try not to be sad,' he reassured them. 'Like the coming of the rains, we are born into this world and receive the precious gift of life. But there are other things, sacred things, that we must speak of now...'

Placing his right hand on the shoulder of each of his two sons in turn, Nachancan instructed them to go at night along the secret mountain tracks he had shown them – Itzamna to the east and Arana to the west – taking their burning torches to light their path. They should be sure to take thick blankets to stay warm.

3

And each in turn should call to the ancient ones for guidance on their special quest.

'When you return,' he told them, 'you must tell me what the ancient ones have shown you, what they have shared with you. Then, and only then, will I name one of you as my chosen successor, as custodian of the Sacred Way...'

The two young men understood what they had to do. For a moment they stood silently, reflecting on the daunting nature of the important task ahead. Then they walked back inside the family hut and across to the hearth where Zafrina had prepared bowls of nourishing food. Taking the warm earthenware bowls in their hands they eagerly devoured the tasty vegetable broth and then silently gathered the blankets and brushwood torches that their mother had put aside for them.

Just as they were preparing to leave, Nachancan called them back beside his bed. There was something else he wanted to tell them. He looked tired and pale but still there was a lingering fire in his dark brown eyes.

'Take care,' he told them, 'to call the ancient ones with all the grace and wisdom that dwells inside your heart. And remember that Grandmother Moon will guide your journey through the night...'

2

AS THEY STEPPED OUTSIDE for the first time they felt the sudden impact of the fresh night air against their warm faces. Huddling inside their blankets and carrying their brushwood torches they emerged from the dense cluster of palm trees that lined the family compound. Then they strode briskly past the rickety wire fence towards the low stone wall that marked the boundary of the family land. Pausing to reflect on the task ahead they glanced back at their homestead, the place where their father lay dying. The steep thatched roof of the stucco hut stood out like a dark sentinel against the star-filled sky.

A cold and penetrating gust was already sweeping up from the lake, bringing with it the distinctive smell of wood-smoke from the scattered settlements further down the mountain. Lights twinkled like little silver stars from the villages dotted alongside the dark face of Lake Atitlán. But Itzamna and Arana knew that their personal quest and challenge lay elsewhere. They embraced and bid farewell to each other and then headed off along the narrow mountain tracks in opposite directions.

Itzamna was stocky and strongly built with a broad chest and heavy, muscular shoulders. His face was round and open, his large oval eyes dark and intense. His wore his black hair pulled back in a long plait that he sometimes tucked inside a red cloth headband. Tonight his plait dangled loose and carefree, swaying in the strong breeze as he hurried along. Two large blankets were slung across his shoulders and he had tucked a small machete into his waistband.

Itzamna was taller and more confident than his younger brother, and he had always taken the lead when they were out on the lake fishing, or in the mountains hunting for tapirs and wild pigs. But tonight as he made his way along the rocky track he felt a sense of foreboding. In itself the night quest held few fears and uncertainties. He knew where the track itself would take him…that it led to an outcrop of sharp rocks and tall leafy trees where he could look out across the lake and summon the ancient ones from the vast, mysterious void of the dark horizon. But tonight he was troubled by the nagging thought that perhaps the spirits would not hear him. He worried that on this particular occasion, for some reason or other, they would choose to remain silent.

When Itzamna arrived at the rocky outcrop he knelt down in a place protected from the persistent, blustery wind, and unfurled one of his blankets on the ground. Then he sat down, cross-legged and silent, huddled himself within the folds of the other blanket and closed his eyes. He breathed deeply and let out a little gasp as he tried to relax and remain calm. From deep within he then prayed to the great ones – to Grandfather Fire who would give him strength to become ever more resilient, and to the Holy Womb Mother, who had given him birth as the much-loved son of Nachancan and Zafrina. Then he prayed to Father Sun, thanking him for his life-sustaining warmth and inspiration and to Mother Mountain, who would protect him during his vigil through the night. Then he offered his heart and soul to the ancestors, bidding them welcome and seeking a clear omen that would illuminate his path in the important times ahead.

The wind was now lapping around his ankles and his mouth felt parched and sore. He was finding it hard to stay warm, hard to stay focused on the important spiritual purpose that had brought him here. Slowly he rose to his feet. He could see the faint and distant outline of the three large volcano peaks across the lake. Black against black….shades of dark expanse tapering off into nothingness… He looked up towards the star-filled sky. Then he held his arms aloft and called for a sign from the ancient ones.

But no sign came. He waited patiently for a response. Still there was no sign. More time passed, but even now no sign was forthcoming. In a mood of silent determination Itzamna turned his attention instead to the elusive, whispering sounds all around him, to the carping calls of the night-birds and to the rustling noises of the small animals scampering in the shrubs and bushes along the craggy forested slopes. Perhaps the ancient ones would speak to him from deep within the earth? Perhaps they would send a guiding song or a spirit-helper that would open a path to the other world and provide the answers he now sought?

But there was only silence, as even the calls of the night-birds and the scurrying noises of the animals abated and then died away. With every passing moment came the sickening realization that there would be no message from the great ones, no guiding message that Itzamna could take back to his father...

As dawn broke Itzamna felt the tightness in his belly, a tightness like a rigid knot of thick rope sapping the very strength and life from his aching bones. He was bitterly disappointed. He was devastated that the gods and spirit-helpers had not spoken to him or offered guidance during this testing and difficult time. Slowly he made his way back along the narrow mountain track, saddened by the thought that he had no vision to share, no insight to impart... nothing he could tell his father to show that he, Itzamna, should be the chosen one...

When he finally arrived back at the stone boundary wall that marked the edge of the family land, he chose not to return to the compound. Instead he continued along the narrow dirt path that led down the side of the mountain into the small village of Xocomil which nestled neatly beside the lake. Zafrina had already found a place for herself on the grey paved stones in the marketplace and was busy arranging the vegetables and woven fabrics that she had brought down to sell. But Itzamna quickly passed her by, pretending not to notice her, and walked sullenly across to the other side of the square, over in the direction of the old colonial church of Santo Tomás.

7

Nevertheless, Zafrina had caught a brief glimpse of her elusive son as he slid quickly out of view behind the other vendors and fruit carts, and she knew he had returned from his night vigil with a heavy heart. For the moment she would say nothing to Nachancan but she knew that when Itzamna next spoke with him there would be only disappointment.

Meanwhile Itzamna was shuffling aimlessly among the fruit and vegetable traders in the busy marketplace. He knew many of the people down here but he was doing everything he could to avoid catching their attention. He knew if someone were to pull him aside now he would react angrily and aggressively. It was better this way... better to remain silent and pass through the crowd unnoticed.

But Itzamna had not gone unnoticed. Not only had Zafrina seen him sneak past but Pedro Delgado had noticed him as well. He looked on with curiosity as the young man made his way across the market plaza in the direction of the church.

Pedro was a slim, energetic man in his early sixties with a shock of bushy grey-white hair, pale olive skin and an expressive smile. Today he was wearing his regular clothing, an old red and black checked shirt and light-weight cotton trousers held up by a simple rope belt. He looked more like a town worker than a priest in the local church. Pedro was popular with everyone who knew him and that meant most of the people who lived and worked in Xocomil and the neighbouring region around the lake.

Widely admired for his cheerful, optimistic outlook, he had worked tirelessly for many years as officiating priest in the Church of Santo Tomás. What endeared him to so many in the Mayan community was his willingness to go among the local people and accept them on their own terms. While he would always openly declare his own perspectives on the Christian faith he would never urge others to convert to the spiritual path of Rome. Pedro willingly conceded that the Mayan people had their own sacred traditions and that these traditions had served them well for countless generations, long before the coming of the Spanish colonial powers. Pedro considered the call of religion in entirely human terms. He was there to serve, he was there to help. And he was always willing to encourage those who seemed downcast and dejected...

'How are things with you today?' he asked with a cautious smile, as the young man came closer. He had known Nachancan and Zafrina for many years and had taken a keen interest in their children, especially since his own wife had died all those long years ago and he had none of his own to care for.

'Have you been helping your mother over there in the marketplace...?'

Itzamna remained silent, his face turned aside to avoid eye-contact. Pedro could see that something was seriously troubling him. Without saying a word he led him across to an old wooden bench beside the colonnade.

As they sat down together the morning sun streamed across the market square, brightening all the colours. The fruits and vegetables and large piles of handwoven fabrics glistened like little jewels of light.

'My father sent me on a mission,' said Itzamna finally, breaking his silence.

'My task was to gain wisdom and guidance from the sacred ones. But they turned their backs on me. They did not wish to speak to me...'

'They did not wish to speak to you?'

'They chose not to appear at all...'

'What did you think they would tell you?' asked the priest, hoping to draw him out a little.

'I thought they might encourage me... support me,' said Itzamna, lifting his head just a little as he continued to look down at the ground.

Pedro was listening attentively. He noticed that the boy's hands were quivering as he spoke and he wondered how he could help.

'I was looking for a sign, some sort of sign. Something I could bring back and tell my father...'

He crossed his arms and looked down sullenly at his lap.

'...so he would name me and not Arana as his successor. So I would become the new custodian of the Calendar Wheel...'

Pedro nodded silently. He had some feeling for what the boy was talking about even though he had never taken part in any of the shaman ceremonies. He also understood Itzamna's rivalry with his brother. It was a natural thing among the young Mayan men, after all.

Pedro appreciated that Nachancan was highly regarded, both as a shaman and as a leader of his people, but he had never sought to probe further than mutual respect demanded. He was well aware that the Mayan shamans had their own approach to everything they considered sacred and he had never wished to encroach on territory where he did not belong.

'And now...?' asked Pedro, pondering the outcome.

'Now I must forsake the path of my father,' said Itzamna solemnly. 'Now I must leave it all behind ...'

Itzamna looked back across the marketplace and got ready to leave.

He was grateful for Father Delgado's interest and support but right now he wanted to be alone.

'There's always a place for you here at the Mission,' said the priest reassuringly. 'I'll always be here if you want to come back and talk about it...'

But Itzamna was already making his way along the cobbled street. Pedro watched as he merged into the shadows of the narrow pathway that led down towards the lake. Itzamna was going somewhere, anywhere, where he could spend some time alone and reflect on what he should do next.

3

THAT EVENING ITZAMNA MADE HIS WAY up the steep mountain path and returned home. As he entered the hut he noticed immediately that they had moved Nachancan out of the open shelter and into another bed inside, to help keep the old man warm. Now his father took pride of place in the most central part of the compound. He still looked frail and tired but he seemed happy enough with everyone bustling all around him, watching out for his every need. He was propped up against a large pillow, huddled inside a thick woollen blanket that had been tucked up around his ears. His thin arms protruded from the folds and he was eagerly devouring a bowl of hot broth that Zafrina had cooked up for him. Malinali was there too, sitting quietly on a blanket beside the hearth, but there was no sign of Arana. Clearly he had not yet returned...

His father beckoned across to him, welcoming him back. He was keen to hear what his son had to say.

Itzamna cleared his throat and sat down beside his father on a small wooden stool. But he did not look at him directly. Instead he looked up towards the flickering shadows in the thatched roof...away from the gaze of those dark questioning eyes...

'The great ones did not speak to me,' said Iztamna dejectedly. It was a struggle to get the words out amidst such strong expectations.

'No omen came. The ancient ones offered no guidance...'

Nachancan remained silent. He'd had a feeling that this might happen. He nodded and then looked away, pondering how best to respond. He could sense his son's sadness and intense regret. He could feel the lingering hurt and pain that had burrowed deep inside his soul and he knew it was best not to dwell on these things right now. Better just to let the matter rest...

'Have some soup to warm your belly,' he said, making light of his son's concerns.

Zafrina brought across another bowl of broth and Itzamna accepted it willingly. It had been a long time since he had eaten anything and an aching, hollow feeling had been gnawing away inside him all day.

'Arana has not yet returned,' said the old man. 'He's out there somewhere...'

After sipping his hot soup with the wooden spoon his mother had given him Itzamna retrieved the last scraps of tomato and squash and pushed them into his mouth with his fingers, savouring the taste. But he knew he wouldn't stay long. In the morning he would gather some food and blankets, slip back into the village and then maybe go and live by himself in the abandoned hut he had discovered, out along the shoreline of the lake. He would feel better out there. Soon his strength would come back and he would find his own way forward. This would clearly be a parting of the ways...

After he had finished eating he went across to his hammock which he had hitched up in the furthest corner of the compound. He much preferred sleeping in the hammock to nestling in blankets and mats on the cold dirt floor. Up there in his hammock he could lose himself in his thoughts as he swayed gently from side to side, staring up at the thatched roof and slipping away slowly into the deep, fleeting shadows of his future hopes and dreams.

When he awoke in the morning Malinali was standing beside him. She had taken hold of one of his hands as it dangled from the hammock, grasping it in her warm fingers. She was smiling affectionately but at the same time she understood the deep pain he was feeling, the gaping wound inflicted on him as the ancient ones had chosen not to heed his call. And even though he hadn't told her directly, she already sensed that he would soon be leaving. Malinali understood his need now to find his own path in the world, a path that might even take him away from the helper-spirits and ancient ones who watched over their people. She had brought him a plate of fruit, some slices of freshly cut avocado, and a scattering of nuts.

Itzamna truly loved his young sister. And she was becoming ever more beautiful by the day. Her deep brown eyes were warm and engaging, her skin smooth and golden brown. She was becoming more shapely too – she already had the elegant body of a young woman, ripening with life, and was no longer the frolicking giggly girl he used to play with in the cornfields and down near the fishing boats beside the lake. Most of all he loved her spirit, which was a spirit of warm and generous under- standing. She would make a fine wife and companion for one of the lucky boys in the village when the time came for her to have a family of her own...

But for the moment he just smiled back at her, knowing there was a strong bond between them and that right now words could not express the powerful emotions he had been struggling with. He knew she would always be there when he needed someone to talk to, someone to confide in.

'I found an abandoned hut that nobody's using, down by the lake shore,' he told her. 'One of the walls is badly damaged and the thatched roof has sections that are broken, but it will be all right to live in. I won't be far away....'

He looked again into her smiling golden eyes and then he gave her a hug with his strong broad arms.

'You'll know where to find me,' he whispered. 'You'll know where to come if you need me.'

4

EARLY NEXT DAY ZAFRINA AND MALINALI went down to the marketplace leaving Nachancan once again in his special vantage place beneath the shelter where he could gaze out at the lake. They didn't like leaving him alone but Nachancan had reassured them and told them he was feeling fine...better than yesterday, when he had felt weak and tired for most of the day. But this was another day, and everything seemed good for the moment. A small green and yellow bird was chirping away a short distance from where he was resting. It was an amusing distraction just listening to its cheerful song...

The sun had risen high in the sky and the lake was now a soft and diffuse pale blue, fading off into a haze of silver around the shoreline. Again Nachancan could see the fishermen scattered out across the lake like little black insects but he had to shield his face with his wrinkled hand to avoid the penetrating glare of the sun. It would hurt his eyes if he looked out too long. Even so, he was not complaining. He enjoyed these quiet and solitary times for he could gather his thoughts and reflect on the many good and happy times that had marked his long life.

Suddenly he heard a rustling noise in the adjoining room, the sound of footsteps shuffling towards him. Feeling suddenly anxious he stretched around, craning his neck to see... Arana had returned...

The old man was pleased to welcome him back and waved him over. Arana looked radiant and uplifted, as if he had come through some sort of ordeal. Nachancan noticed there was an unusual light in his eyes. There were also scratch-marks on his skin where he had perhaps lain on hard, rocky ground or cut himself on sharp protruding branches. Even so, his clothes seemed intact and he looked surprisingly alert after three nights away in the mountains. He was still carrying his blankets and a small bundle of food. Nachancan called him over to sit beside him on his bed.

Arana sat down beside his father, looking out at Lake Atitlán. A light breeze had come up from the water and the air smelt fresh and clean.

'I spent three nights on the mountain tracks,' he said quickly, knowing full well that his father would want to know right away what had happened while he was gone.

'On the first night, I prayed to the ancient ones in the way you showed me. I prayed to Chac and then to Kinich Ahau and then to Kukulcan and, of course, to Ix Chel... Naturally, I asked for their blessing and their protection...'

'Did you feel scared up there on the mountain?' asked the old man. '...up there on the mountain, all alone ...?'

'To begin with I did feel scared, ' said Arana, acknowledging his father's concern. 'Once I heard the rustling of a snake quite close in the long grass, but then it went away and it was all right after that...'

'And then...?'

'During the daylight hours I spent most of the time wandering around on top of the cliffs. All the time I was away I saw no-one else from the village, no-one else I knew. And yet I could feel while I was up there that Kukulcan was purifying me, blowing away the demons with his air-breath, blowing away the spirits of illness and fear. Then in the middle of the day I lay down on a large smooth rock. I was drawn towards it.... it was warm from the sun and the warmth soothed my back. And then I felt Kinich Ahau pouring his sunlight into my chest, pouring his light straight into my soul. And it was changing me... making me stronger. Later I saw him...'

'You saw him...?'

'When I opened my eyes, there was a large red and yellow macaw. Right up close... in a tree, nearby. Up close, with its

15

large, sharp beak and glistening feathers. Looking down at me with his glinting eyes...'

'And you knew it was Kinich Ahau...?'

'I knew it was him. He spoke his name. I knew he had come to guide me...'

Nachanchan smiled quietly to himself. This was indeed a good omen. He had never told Arana that the sun god Kinich Ahau sometimes transformed into a brightly coloured macaw. This was something Arana had now discovered for himself.

'And did you make an offering to Kinich Ahau ...?'

'I did,' replied Arana. 'I gathered seeds and aromatic leaves, and flowers from a nearby ceiba tree, and I made an offering to him. I made a small fire from the embers that were still smouldering and as the smoke from the leaves rose high into the sky, I thanked him for visiting me and guiding me up there on the mountain...'

Nachancan rested his hand on Arana's shoulder. He was well pleased by what his son was telling him.

'With the passing of the daylight, with the rising of the moon... what happened next?'

'I prayed to Ix Chel. It was a star-filled night. The moon was full and it was light all about. I could see quite well, far off into the distance. I didn't need my torch....'

Nachancan was listening attentively.

' .. and then she came down from the stars. Ix Chel came down from the heavens along a path lit on both sides by rows of glistening silver lights. And then she hovered above me, up there on the mountain...'

Arana looked up at his father to make sure that he was listening to everything he had to say.

'I was scared at first because she was a really ugly old woman and not at all what I expected. She had wild and crazy hair that pointed in all directions, and she had green pointed teeth that looked like little poisoned arrowheads. I was really frightened

16

by her. In one hand she was holding a twisting, writhing snake and I thought it might reach out and bite me. She was wearing a skirt made up of old grey bones that had been crudely stitched together with pieces of twine. Her breasts were flat and wrinkled and hung down over me, and she was glaring down at me with her sharp green fangs....'

He paused for a moment and then continued.

'But then I noticed, in her other hand, she was holding a large jug of water. Suddenly she poured it all over me, drenching me, drowning me, cleansing me, washing me into the earth...'

'And then ...?'

'When I opened my eyes, she was no longer a frightening old witch but a beautiful young woman. She had changed entirely and she was different from any woman I have ever seen before... There were glistening stars in her eyes, and her skin was smooth... like finely beaten silver. Her hair fell in braids like long strands of moonlight. Her breasts were full and firm, her smile was radiant like the full moon... She placed her hand upon my forehead and then she blessed me. And she gave me her secret name, the name I should use to call her in the sacred times. The name I should use to protect families under her care and bring rain for the crops....'

'And these are the things that happened to you, up there on the mountain?'

The old man was impressed by what he was hearing. Powerful things had been happening in the time he'd been away...

'Yes... but that's not all,' said Arana. There was still more to tell...

'On the third night the sun god came back to see me again. He came down out of the darkness high above Lake Atitlán. He came down out of the night sky and glided like a bird across the waves of the lake and then he walked right up the side of the cliff-face to where I was standing. And this time he looked very

17

different. He had a head like a jaguar and the body of a warrior, with a long spear and a hunting knife. But I knew it was him, because he uttered his name again, right there on the mountain. He came right up to me, right up close. He was so close that I could see the heaving of his chest, feel his hot breath against my cheek. And then he carefully cut a small mark in my chest and allowed three drops of blood to fall down onto the earth. And he said he would protect me from this time onwards...'

Arana pulled his shirt open and let Nachancan see the small bloody mark on his chest.

'That is indeed a good sign,' said Nachanchan. He was well pleased that the sun god had made himself known in this way.

'And there was one other thing he warned me about,' said Arana, continuing his account...

'He told me we must be wary of a dark shaman, a dark warrior and sorcerer, who would try with all his heart and strength to fight and block us as we opened the path to the Sacred Way...'

'Did Kinich Ahau give you the name of this dark shaman...?' asked the old man.

He was anxious now...

'The sun god told me his name. His name is Ahmok. He lives by himself in a secluded hut on the other side of the lake...'

Ahmok...*Ahmok*... Nachancan knew the dreaded shaman well. He had faced him many times in the spirit-world, fought desperate battles to retrieve the smitten souls of village folk that had been snatched away across the lake and then held hostage in dark, secluded caves beneath the earth. Ahmok also took pleasure in despatching his demon-arrows of disease and mayhem whenever he could. He would set village huts afire through his sorcery, and frighten the women and children...

Suddenly Nachancan looked pale and tired. He was disturbed by what his son was telling him.

'Speak of this to no-one,' he said, the skin tightening around his mouth.

18

'Later I will tell you more about this dark shaman. Later I will tell you more about what he stands for and why we must always guard against him... Of all the adversaries you will face in the future, he is the one you should beware of when you open the path to the Sacred Way...'

Despite his warning about Ahmok, Arana knew when he heard these words that his father had already made his choice. He knew then that he, Arana, would be named as his father's successor. That he would be given the role of guarding the Calendar Wheel and opening the path to the Sacred Way. That from this time onwards his life would be given over entirely to serving the protector gods and goddesses of the land and sky, of the cornfields and the lake...

Arana glanced across at the shimmering waters and then looked back at his frail and aging father, at the great and venerable shaman in whose footsteps he would soon follow. He was a good man... a father one could truly be proud of. Arana knew a great honour had been bestowed on him, and he was deeply grateful.

5

WHEN ZAFRINA AND MALINALI returned Nachancan called them over to sit beside him on the bed. Then he leaned his head back against the pillow and told them that the choice had been made. Arana would be his successor. The ancient ones had made their will known up there on the mountain. And he, Nachancan, was happy to give his younger son his blessing.

But there was still an important duty for Nachancan to fulfil. He knew he must now go urgently with Arana to the cave of the Calendar Wheel and show him the ritual he must perform as the new custodian of the Sacred Way. At the same time he would share with him the secrets that had been passed down from father to son through countless generations. These were the secrets of his shaman-lineage that would be understood with the coming of the final time.... the final day on the Calendar Wheel when, as the ancient ones had foretold, the world would change forever.

Shortly after daybreak Nachancan rose stiffly from his bed, splashed some cold water on his face from an earthen jug and braced himself for his final journey up the mountain. His strength had been fading these last few days but he knew he must muster all his reserves of energy and personal power. It was now time to show his son the secret things revealed only to the custodian of the sacred path.

Arana helped his father dress, finding him a clean pair of trousers and assisting him as he pulled his woven shirt up over his head. Then he went to get him a broad-rimmed straw hat that would shield his eyes from the powerful light of the sun. As they walked outside together, Arana allowed the old man to lean up against his shoulder so he wouldn't slip and fall. Passing by the clump of palm trees and dense shrubs that lined the family compound they made their way towards the rocky wall that marked the boundary of the family land. Out here the air smelt fresh and invigorating. Nachancan paused and took a deep breath. This was an important day, perhaps the most important day remaining while he was still alive in this world.

Turning in the direction of Panajachel, some distance away around the lake, they walked along the rocky path until they came to a place where a large bush with an abundance of purple flowers marked a bend in the track. Nachancan gestured to Arana, telling him that they would now leave the familiar path and make their way through an expanse of tall grass and shrubs, up a steep incline towards to a rocky ledge in the distance. There they would scramble over some rocks and join another narrow path, a little known track that led up to the more distant reaches of the mountain.

Arana moved on ahead, slashing at the tall grass with his sharp machete and cutting away any obstructing branches that blocked their path. Then they scrambled together up a cluster of large crumbling rocks and reached the narrow path that the old man had said would lead up to the secret cave. As they looked back down the mountain, surveying the path they had taken, Nachancan took another deep breath and steadied his gaze. The lake seemed much further away now, almost hidden from view, and the shrubs and bushes along this track were denser and more overgrown than he remembered.

'I brought you up here once before,' said the old man, regaining his balance and looking out into the haze of the midday sun.

'I brought you here with Itzamna when you were just young boys...'

Arana couldn't recall the time. This part of the mountain was far away from the familiar walking tracks. It was not a place he would ever think of exploring. Even here, where they were right now, the track seemed to lead nowhere in particular. Further up the mountain the rocks looked jagged and uneven and there were no obvious indentations in the side of the cliff-face.... no obvious signs of a passage leading deep inside the mountain.

'You can't see the entrance to the cave from down here,' said the old man, anticipating Arana's thoughts.

'The entrance can only be seen when you are right up there, near that furthest ledge...'

He pointed with his outstretched hand.

'And, even then, you may only enter if the gods allow it...'

Nachancan smiled as he said this, and Arana thought in turn of Ahmok, the dark shaman, fighting his magical battles with his father. Pitting his sorcery against the timeless magic of the Sacred Way...

They pressed on further. Arana could tell that his father was struggling, but together they moved on up the path, step by step, pausing every now and then so the old man could catch his breath and recover some of his strength.

Then, finally, they were there.

Two angular basalt rocks, wedged up against each other like a portal, marked a narrow passageway that opened out onto a level area edged with smaller rocks and little tufts of grass. Shafts of soft sunlight fell across the large basalt rocks. And there, off to one side beside a large unfamiliar bush that partly blocked his view, Arana could see the opening to the cave. A cluster of flat paving stones had been wedged into the earth, marking the entrance.

They edged their way into the open space in front of the cave and Nachancan indicated that they should sit down on the ground. This was a good place to talk.

For a while they sat silently, aware of the ancient memories that seemed to linger in this place. Nachancan was the first to speak.

'All the shamans in our family line have come to this cave,' said the old man. 'It is a place known only to us, and it must remain a secret and sacred place...'

He picked up a small twig and drew two circles in the dirt, one within the other.

'What marks us apart is that we are custodians for two sacred paths. The first is the sacred way of the Calendar Wheel that contains the wheel of the Tzolkin and the wheel of the Haab. The Tzolkin dwells within the Haab and together the cycles of the seasons move forward. These wheels remain alive, they remain in motion, only when we honour the great gods and goddesses...'

Nachancan looked across at Arana to make sure he was listening closely. He was well aware that time was precious, that these things had to be addressed now...

'The wheels remain in motion when we make offerings to the great gods and goddesses on the sacred, ceremonial days that are dedicated to them and to them alone... when we call their secret names....'

He paused for a moment to emphasize his point.

'It has always been this way...'

Arana had heard already about the Tzolkin and the Haab. He knew that the Tzolkin ceremonial wheel turned through a cycle of 260 days and that the Haab contained the eighteen sacred symbols of the sun, each representing the passage of twenty days. In this way the eighteen symbols on the Haab wheel accounted for 360 days, all of them governed by the power of light. But the other five days that remained in each year – the five days known as Vayeb – were considered auspicious and dangerous times... when souls could be lost and dark forces might prevail.

'When we go inside the cave,' said the old man, 'you will see the Calendar Wheel marked out upon the ground. You will see it there, carved carefully and reverently in stone, with the Tzolkin and the Haab and the sacred names of the Great Ones. This is the Wheel of the Sacred Way. It is alive... it is holy...'

He looked up at his son and could see he was listening attentively.

23

'As I have already told you, we are custodians for two sacred paths and this is what sets us apart. This is why we have a special duty... not only to our people but also to the ancient ones who have given us our life and brought us forth into the world....'

He drew another crooked line in the dirt, indicating the eastern shores of the Mayan lands and the coastline further north.

'When the Spanish powers, the pale-faced devils, came in their boats they landed here on the northern shores. And through treachery and cunning they captured the Temple of the Sun in Teotihuacan. Later the soldiers came south into our lands. The devil, Alvarado, was the scourge of our people...'

Arana knew already of Pedro de Alvarado, the crazed and bloodthirsty soldier in Cortez's army, who had brought terror and destruction to Guatemala. A great battle had been fought west of Lake Atitlán in the region around Quetzaltenango. It was here that the native peoples had been defeated, the land overrun by the conquering invaders.

'Have you heard of the one called Malinche?' asked Nachancan, looking across at his son.

Arana shook his head.

'Malinche was a young woman who spoke the language of the Maya and the language of our brothers, the Aztecs. She won the affections of the conqueror, Cortez. She betrayed our people to the Spanish devils. It was she who made it possible for the destruction and terror to take place. And it was her brother, the evil shaman known as Kaak, who brought the dark powers, the dark magic, into our lands and here among our people.'

He paused for a moment as if to reinforce his point. Then he drew a vertical line with little crosses marked out at different points.

'The one we know as Ahmok is in the shaman-line that comes down from Malinche and Kaak. He belongs to their cursed lineage. It is he who has brought the dark forces to Lake Atitlán...'

'How could this have happened?' asked Arana. He was surprised that the people of Teotihuacan could have been so easily betrayed.

'At first our northern brothers welcomed the Spanish devils,' said Nachancan slowly, looking down at his markings in the dirt. 'They welcomed them at our shores because the pale-faced ones had come at a time considered holy on the sacred Calendar Wheel. They thought that the pale-faced god, the great feathered serpent they called Quetzalcoatl, was returning to their people...'

Arana was still puzzled by what his father was telling him.

'Who was this pale-faced god?' he asked. 'Why were they hoping for his return...?'

'Many, many years ago,' said the old man, 'a wise and well-travelled teacher came to our shores. He arrived here in a boat, from another land. He had long hair and a brown beard and a pale face. He did not look like our people. But he spoke of love and peace and urged the warriors who fought battles against each other to put down their weapons. He urged them to live among themselves in peace and harmony. He urged them to live like true brothers in this land...'

Arana was listening attentively to what his father was telling him.

'The pale-faced one carried with him a box carved from wood. Inside was a small piece of cloth on which he had written his sacred teachings. He said that these teachings had come from the sky, from his father who lived among the Ancient Ones. He said it was good to follow the path of the Sacred Way and that our people should follow this path until the end of time...'

'Until the end of time...?'

'Until the final day which is marked out for our people on the sacred Calendar Wheel,' said the old man. 'The pale-faced one told our people that on that day the world would change forever...'

'And what happened next?' asked Arana. He was fascinated

by what his father was telling him.

'The pale-faced teacher journeyed next to the southern lands, and spoke also with our brothers there, urging peace and love and an end to the fighting and blood sacrifice. Then he returned once again to our people. Finally he left from the western shore, sailing away once again in a boat across the sea, away to the distant horizon...'

Arana sensed there was more to tell.

'When the pale-faced one, whom we know as Kukulcan, vanished with the wind, we too hoped for his return. But he left behind something for us to keep, something we should guard as sacred and precious...'

'And what was that?' asked Arana.

'His wooden box,' said the old man. 'The wooden box containing his teaching of love and peace...the teaching in his wooden box, which also told of the Second Coming at the end of time...'

'The Second Coming of Kukulcan?'

'Perhaps...' said his father. '...but it is written in words which our people cannot read. It is written in words which we cannot understand...'

'And where is the wooden box now?'

'It is hidden in the cave behind you,' said Nachancan. 'We have kept it secret and hidden away since the pale-faced teacher first walked among our people. And now you have become the custodian. Now it is your duty to guard the secret teaching... the teaching of the Sacred Way.'

Nachancan got up slowly from the ground and gestured to Arana to follow him into the cave. Just inside the entrance, he lit a large candle that had been left in an earthen bowl. Then he went further inside and lit several other candles around the edge of the cave so Arana could see more clearly.

The sacred Calendar Wheel was marked out in large stone sections placed carefully on the ground, just as his father had told him. The designs had been intricately carved and took up most of the floor of the cave. Arana bent down and looked more closely. He recognised the names of the different days in the Tzolkin wheel : Ahau, Imix, Ik, Akbal, Kan...and on through the cycle to Etznab and Caunac. Then he looked up at the walls of the cave. All around him he could see vivid and carefully painted images of the Ancient Ones: the sun god Kinich Ahau shown in the form of a jaguar; Itzamna, ruler of the heavens, in whose honour his brother had been named; Yumil Kaxob, god of corn and flowers; the moon goddess Ix Chel whom he had encountered during his night-vigil; Kekchi, god of mountains and valleys; Ah Puch, lord of the underworld and Chac, god of rain. Kukulcan, the much beloved god of the wind, was there too. Arana wondered whether, one day, Kukulcan would return to this cave and share his secret teachings once again. If so, he hoped he would be here to share in the honour of welcoming him back among his people...

Nachancan pointed to a bowl of white flower petals in the furthest corner of the cave.

'East is the direction of new life. When you place these petals from the sacred ceiba tree along the rim of the Calendar Wheel, commencing in the East, you bring the wheel to life. When you utter the secret names that are written here on the stones, you bring sacred power to the people. The names, themselves, are power....'

Nachancan looked reverently at the intricate stone carvings beneath his feet.

'With these sacred and secret names you can call the seasons to flow, you can call the spirits of unborn babies to enter the womb of the Earth Mother. With these sacred and secret names you can call rain to fall, nourishing the corn and other crops and you can call the winds to abate, allowing safe passage for the fishermen out on the lake...'

Arana was inspired by what his father was sharing with him.

27

It was indeed a magical, holy place.

'We will speak further of your ritual tasks,' said Nachancan, 'but now I want to show you Kukulcan's gift, the treasured gift I spoke of earlier...'

He walked back into the depths of the cave, reached up onto a small ledge, and brought forth the ancient wooden box. It was rectangular in shape and had been crudely assembled from sections of thick, dark-grained wood. Arana estimated it measured around four hand-widths across. Stains and weathered scratch marks were visible around the edge and one corner had been slightly damaged; perhaps it had been dropped at some time in the past. But the wooden lid seemed to be intact and was fastened to the box with a simple metal clasp...

Nachancan pulled back the lid.

Inside Arana could see fragments of what looked like stiff cloth or parchment, which at one time must have been joined together in a single scroll. Now it had begun to fray around the edges and was already fracturing into pieces. In the dim candle-light he could make out lines of curious angular markings. The script was completely unfamiliar, quite unlike anything he had seen in the local school library, or in the Church of Santo Tomás.

'And this is the gift from Kukulcan?' he asked in amazement. It was strange and overwhelming seeing this completely unfamiliar script... these sacred and secret writings left here by the mysterious pale faced visitor, all those countless years ago.

The old man nodded.

'When you come here to make your special offerings...,' said Nachancan, '...when you call upon the gods and goddesses whose secret names have now been revealed to you, take care at the same time to place this gift from Kukulcan at the very heart of the Calendar Wheel.'

He pointed down at its centre.

'When you do that, when you honour Kukulcan in this way, the Path of the Sacred Way can be opened. The path can be made open for the Ancient One who approaches us even now. Even now, as we speak...'

'...Even now?' asked Arana

'Even now,' said his father. 'Even now, as the final time draws closer...'

6

ZAFRINA AND MALINALI had stayed behind in the compound. They understood that the men had their sacred functions to perform and today Zafrina and her daughter were doing what they often did when they were left alone at home. Zafrina had taken out her loom and was busy weaving fabric in the traditional patterns of her people, the patterns which marked out the distinctive style of Xocomil from all the other towns and villages around the lake. During the last few days she had been making a new shirt for Arana and a decorative headband for her daughter, one with birds and rainbows and brightly coloured flowers. At the same time Malinali was busy mixing up some corn, tomatoes and squash with a few chunks of pumpkin to make a fine *pulic* stew. She would cook it up and share it around when the men returned just before nightfall.

But just like the male shamans of the village, the shaman-women of Xocomil also had their own sacred duties to attend to. As Zafrina was weaving her patterns she remembered that she had not yet spoken with Malinali about the oracle. And now, while they were alone by themselves, they could seek guidance from the Lake Mother together... they could search for an omen in the living waters that would show them times of crisis in the days that lay ahead.

Zafrina put down her loom and asked Malinali to come and sit beside her on the woollen rug in front of the hearth.

'Your father believes the ancient ones are calling him now,' she said softly, hinting at the impending sorrow that now haunted her thoughts.

'He already sees the path to Xibalba opening before him in the night sky...'

Malinali nodded silently.

'And who knows...?' she said. 'I am an old woman too. Maybe

the great ones will soon be calling me as well...'

Such an idea was far from Malinali's mind. She hadn't even considered the possibility. It would be an enormous loss when finally both her father and her mother had departed from the land of the living.

She looked up searchingly at her mother, wondering why she was dwelling on these concerns at this particular time.

'I want to show you something,' said Zafrina.

She went across to another part of the main room where she kept several of her own, private possessions and returned with a large earthenware bowl. Then she placed it on the woollen rug between them so Malinali could see what she was talking about.

'This is something only women perform and this is a special bowl, used only for this purpose. It has been handed down through many generations, from grandmother down to mother and then on to daughter...'

She ran her hand around its edge, admiring the decorative motifs marked out against the brown textured surface.

'This bowl was given to me by my grandmother Nhutalu, who loved me very much and guided me throughout her long life. Now I am passing it on to you...'

Zafrina reached across to a nearby earthen jug and filled the bowl with water.

'Everything filled with water flows with the blessing of life itself,' she said, choosing her words carefully, '... and we who have been nominated as guardians are drawn towards the goddess of the waters. When we enter her realm we learn to see the world around us as it truly is. Through her guidance we can also learn to see the world as it will soon become...'

'As it will soon become...?'

Malinali looked into her mother's wise and loving eyes. She always felt safe when she was alone with her mother and she trusted her completely. She knew, too, that her mother was every bit as strong and wise as her father. Strong and wise in her own

31

special way, in her own special manner...

'When this water is blessed by the Lake Mother, I can see into it like a mirror. When this water is blessed in this way, my eyes are truly opened...'

Zafrina began to hum gently. Then she closed her eyes and began to pray, sending her prayers to the heart of the Lake Mother, goddess of the waters.

Zafrina sat quietly. Her eyes remained closed but when she finally opened them Malinali could see that she was looking out in a different way, looking out in a magical way that opened her spirit to other worlds beyond...

Malinali watched carefully as her mother cast her gaze down into the bowl.

Soon the omen was clear.

'Your beloved father has been summoned to Xibalba. He will leave us before daybreak tomorrow,' she said softly, in little more than a whisper. There was more than a hint of sorrow and regret in her voice, but there was nothing she could do to prevent it. The ancient ones had decreed that this was the time...

She had witnessed this omen once before, and now it had been confirmed yet again. Within the crystal waters of the oracle bowl she had seen the spirit of her husband rise up above the lake, and she had heard the words come forth from the lips of the Lake Mother herself. And she knew then that her beloved Nachancan would soon be journeying towards the home of the ancient ones, journeying along the starlit path through the night sky...

When Zafrina finally turned her gaze away from the bowl, Malinali could see that tears were streaming down her mother's lined and wrinkled cheeks. But she knew her mother would come through all her grief and loss and still remain strong.

Wiping the tears from her eyes Zafrina passed the bowl across to Malinali, inviting her to take it.

'Use this bowl to call the Lake Mother when you need to be with her. Fill it first with fresh water. Then sit quietly and pray to the Lake Mother for guidance... Call her to your side... When you feel she is there beside you, protecting you and guiding you, open your eyes slowly... Then you can enter her world and see what she wishes to share with you...'

She smiled knowingly at her daughter.

'When you do that, the Lake Mother will open your eyes in a different way. She will tell you through the waters what you wish to see and know...'

7

ARANA AND NACHANCAN arrived back just as the last rays of fading sunlight were receding across the lake. Nachancan was tired and wanted to rest his sore and aching limbs. Arana helped him undress and led him across to his bed. Soon the old man was tucked inside his warm blankets.

Zafrina brought him a bowl of warm pulic stew. She had placed it on a small wooden tray, surrounded by a circle of flower petals. They both understood what this signified but this was not the time for sadness or regret. They both knew this would be their last evening together around the hearth.

Nachancan was pleased that Arana had understood his ritual tasks for opening the Sacred Way. They had spoken further of these things as they walked back down from the cave. The old man felt sure that Arana would live to see the return of Kukulcan, even if he himself would not be here to witness it. The Calendar Wheel had marked it all out before them. The final time would be with them soon. The sacred living stones of the Calendar Wheel were turning in their cycles, marking out the days for the coming revelation...

The old man savoured every last taste in his hearty meal. It was good, indeed, to still be here and he could share this special time with Zafrina, Malinali and Arana. He was sad, though, that no-one had heard from Itzamna since he had skulked away to live by himself down beside the lake. No doubt his oldest son would find his own path when the ancient ones saw that he was ready.

When the meal was finished they sat quietly together and Zafrina lit a single candle. Then they made a prayer for the good times they had shared and for the blessings which had come to their family — blessings from Itzamna and Ix Chel, from Chac and from Kukulcan whose secrets the old man had guarded through all these years as custodian of the sacred cave. Then they prayed finally to Ah Puch who would soon come for Nachancan from the netherworld beyond the sky. Ah Puch would accompany him to the land beyond the living, leading him far away through the night stars to Xibalba. And there the old man would be welcomed by the ancient ones who knew he had served them well.

When they had completed their prayers Arana offered the old man a small cup of *cuxa* which would help him sleep better through the night. Arana held it up to his dry lips so he could sip at it gently And then, when the candle had finally burnt down to ash, they all went away to rest, knowing in their hearts that in the final hours of darkness, before the coming of the dawn, Ah Puch would have been there amongst them.

When Zafrina awoke early next morning she went straight across to where Nachancan had been sleeping. As the oracle had foretold, she could see immediately that his spirit had departed, that Ah Puch had come for him in the night. Although his eyes were closed and he looked peaceful and content, his skin was cold and moist and bore the certain mark of death. Only then, as she placed her warm hand against his cold, immobile face did Zafrina allow her tears to flow freely. Only then as she dissolved into grief did she allow the mounting wave of sorrow to rise up and overwhelm her. Soon she was wailing and sobbing heavily, mourning the loss of her precious Nachancan, her dear friend and beloved husband who had been closest to her heart through all their many long years together.

As Zafrina's sobbing and wailing echoed through the walls of the small family compound, Arana and Malinali awoke with a start. Quickly they rushed to her side. And as they held her in their arms, comforting her and sharing in her sorrow, they all knew that the old man was gone forever. It would be a different time from this point onwards...

Later, when they were able to muster enough strength to fight away their tears, they moved Nachancan across to his place beneath the shelter, to the special vantage point where in his last few days he had enjoyed gazing out across the lake. Arana brought out the old man's medicine bundle and laid it down beside him, and Zafrina tucked his favourite woollen blanket close in around his body as a mark of caring and respect. Then they made a circle of white candles around his bed and lit each of them in turn. He would remain here, surrounded by the soft glow of candles, until they took him to the burial place and laid him finally in the earth.

* * *

Leaving Arana to comfort Zafrina, Malinali hurried down towards the lake. She knew she must find Itzamna urgently and tell him what had happened to their father. Quickly she made her way to the edge of the family compound and then scurried down the steep mountain path into Xocomil, taking care not to slip as she darted from one rocky footing to another. Passing by the village square where her mother came so often to sell her fruit and vegetables, Malinali ran quickly down the small side street that led towards the sandy foreshore at the edge of the lake. It was a place where several fishermen had pulled their wooden dugout canoes up onto the beach. Skirting the dugouts she then headed off towards a small neck of land that jutted out into the water, some distance away along the foreshore. Here the land was wild and untamed, overrun by vines and creepers and a dense swathe of palm trees that came down close to the water's edge. Someone had built an old storage hut here many years ago, a hut that had been so badly battered by rain storms and heavy winds that it had fallen into disrepair and had long since been abandoned. Malinali hoped she would find her brother there.

Fighting away the tears as she thought again of her father, Malinali trudged doggedly through the mud and long grass along the edge of the lake. Finally she came to the dark pebble beach that marked the edge of the headland. It was some time since she had been down here. Drawing closer to the crowded palm trees and overgrown vines she peered into the dense, unwelcoming foliage that lined the foreshore. The abandoned hut was just scarcely visible, buried amongst the trees. Had Itzamna really meant it when he said he would come down here to live by himself?

She called out his name.

There was no reply.

She called again.

Still there was no response.

Malinali edged her way slowly through the dense bushes and creepers and made her way up to the edge of the hut. The crumbling stucco wall had already begun to fall away in large sections, exposing a number of rotten wooden poles which somehow still managed to support the sagging thatched roof. She pushed against the flimsy wooden door, peering inside. The room was dark and gloomy and smelt dank and unhealthy, hardly a place where one would choose to live. But she could see her brother across on the other side of the room, asleep in the corner... huddled in a blanket on the dirt floor.

'Itzamna... wake up...!'

Her voice was loud enough to rouse him immediately. Surprised by the unexpected intruder he swung round quickly to face the door. Instinctively he reached for his machete, but then he could see who it was.

'Malinali...?'

He hardly expected to see his sister down here...

She ran towards him, her hands reaching out to embrace him. Then she burst into tears.

Kneeling beside him and allowing him to reach out and hold her in his arms, she wept on his shoulder as she told him that their father had died during the night. How his passing had been peaceful and not unexpected. How Zafrina and Arana were both with him now, back home watching over him...

Itzamna was shocked by the news of his father. He got up quickly from his bed, pulled on his shirt and drew the blanket across the thin palm mat he had been resting on. For a time he just stood there in silence, dazed by what he had been told. He felt sad and troubled at the same time. He was deeply uneasy that he hadn't made it up with his father. There were so many things that had been left unsaid. Now those opportunities were lost forever...

Itzamna brushed his arm up against his face and then ran his fingers through his dark unkempt hair. He felt dirty and unwashed. He didn't want his mother to see him looking like this.

He walked down to the lake and reached down, catching some water in his cupped hands. Then he splashed it onto his face and went back to where Malinali was waiting for him, watching him, wondering what had become of her elder brother to make him want to live this way.

Together they walked back towards the village along the edge of the lake.

Passing the dugout canoes beached along on the foreshore they made their way up towards the market square, up past the old colonial church of Santo Tomás.

'This is where my heart belongs now,' said Itzamna, pointing to the church.

They walked past the stone steps leading up to the main entrance.

'Once I wanted to call on the magic of our gods and ancestors, the gods and goddesses of our people. Once I wanted to be the custodian of the Sacred Way. But not any more...'

Malinali glanced across at him, surprised and puzzled by what he was saying.

'I'm done with all those old superstitions... I no longer believe in them... I'm done with all the old gods and ancestors... I'm done with all of that...'

He kicked a stone to one side with his sandal and then looked up at her, daring her to think otherwise.

But despite his protests, Malinali did not really believe him. She remembered the time three years ago when they had gone with Arana on a cultural exchange programme to New Mexico, when he had spoken with the elders in the Taos pueblo and told them how proud he was of his spiritual heritage... how proud he was to be the eldest son of a revered local shaman. She remembered how he had spoken of his father's achievements and hinted that, one day, he too would become a trusted custodian of the sacred ways of his people.

Malinali watched for further signs of his change of heart as they walked together up the rocky path that led back home. Was he really about to abandon the sacred traditions of his departed father?

8

THREE DAYS LATER they buried Nachancan in a small family plot on a grassy slope facing out across the lake. It had taken time to call in all the distant cousins, friends and relatives who lived in neighbouring villages around the shore. Some had even come in their canoes across the lake.

Finally in a small, dignified procession they brought him up the hill, carrying his body in a painted wooden coffin decorated with brightly-coloured fabrics and clusters of white and yellow flowers. Then, when they had given prayers and thanks for the life of a man greatly revered and now dearly missed, they lowered him into the dark earth and carefully placed his medicine bundle and a collection of other treasured possessions in close beside his body.

When it was all over they went back down to the house where they spoke of Nachancan's exploits and talked in hushed and reverent tones about his bravery and his vision, about his loyalty and perseverance, about his love for his family and all those around him. They remembered his jokes and how some of the children called him Papa Nacha, which had then become his family nickname. They spoke too about how he had given so much of his life serving as a custodian of the ancient ways. How he had greatly pleased the gods and ancient ones who now would be welcoming him home in his final resting place in Xibalba.

Later, when the friends and relatives had dispersed, Arana drew Itzamna to one side so they could talk directly with each other. He wanted to be sure that they were still friends as well as brothers. Allies and not enemies...

But Itzamna was in no mood to talk. There was something about him that remained sullen and resentful...

Arana understood the hurt that still lingered inside him. He understood how he would be feeling after being passed over as custodian of the Sacred Way. But he wanted to mention something that their father had thought might bring them back together again, both as brothers and as friends.

'There is something you might like to know...' he said hesitantly.

'...something which might surprise you.'

They sat down together on wooden stools beside the hearth.

'But first I must ask...'

He paused for a moment and then continued.

'Malinali told me you have decided to abandon the ancient ways and join the congregation of Santo Tomás....'

'Pedro Delgado is a fine man,' said Itzamna, avoiding a direct response.

'He surely is,' said Arana. 'But does that mean you have to turn your back on everything we have been brought up to believe? Leave behind everything held sacred by our people...?'

Like Malanali, Arana found it difficult to believe that Itzamna could switch his allegiances so completely.

Itzamna seemed defiant.

'Those are the old ways, the ways of the past. Like I said to Malinali, the gods and ancestors don't speak to me anymore. I no longer believe in them...'

He looked down at the floor and then back up at his brother. Arana was watching him intently.

'I have given my heart to the church ... that is where I belong now...'

Arana had to accept what his brother was telling him even though it filled him with dismay. But there was something else as well...

'When I was up there on the mountain Papa Nacha told me other things about the Sacred Way. He told me things I hadn't heard before...'

Itzamna was still listening, his hands folded loosely in his lap.

41

'He told me there was the shaman way, the way of the Sacred Calendar Wheel... of course, that is something we both know. But he also told me about the way of Kukulcan and the secret teaching of the Second Coming... when the shaman way and the Christian way would come together on the final day...'

Itzamna knew nothing of this. This was something his father hadn't shared with him.

'Many years ago, long before the coming of the Spanish powers, a pale-faced teacher, a man from another land, a man with long brown hair and a beard and a message of peace and love, came to these lands...'

'And you think this man was Jesus?' asked Itzamna. The whole idea sounded ridiculous.

'Not Jesus, but his trusted disciple... Santo Tomás...'

Itzamna was intrigued. He urged his brother to continue.

'Santo Tomás was a loyal follower and a close friend of Jesus,' said Arana, relaying to Itzamna what his father had told him. 'He understood Jesus in the special way that close friends understand each other... the way close friends are with one another. Santo Tomás travelled widely, taking the teachings of Jesus to many distant lands. He even came here among our people. Later he sailed away again, back to where he had come from...'

Arana paused to make sure his brother was paying close attention.

'Our people call him Kukulcan...'

'Kukulcan, the wind god...?'

Arana could sense his brother's disbelief, but he was not deterred.

'Kukulcan left our people with a gift, a special secret teaching... a teaching he urged us to guard and respect. And it is here with us still. Our family have served as custodians of this teaching from the earliest times up till now.'

He walked over to the other side of the room and returned with the wooden box. He had brought it back from the cave.

Drawing open the lid, he showed Itzamna the parchment scroll inside.

For the first time his brother was genuinely curious.

'And this is the gift from Santo Tomás?' he asked. 'This is the gift from Kukulcan...?'

'It is,' said Arana. 'This is the gift from Kukulcan, the secret teaching of Santo Tomás. This is the secret teaching of the Second Coming...'

He put the wooden box down carefully on the floor.

For a moment Itzamna was lost for words. He was intrigued by what his brother was telling him but how could he be sure it was true? He would have to get someone else's opinion.... someone who would really know. Someone he could trust...

He looked up at Arana, wondering if he would allow him to take the scroll away for a short time.

'May I show this to Father Delgado?' he asked.

Arana was pleased by his brother's interest. For the first time the lurking anger had begun to wane. Now they were speaking to each other like true brothers and friends. The way it had been before...

'I'm happy for you to show this scroll to Father Delgado,' he said, passing the box across. 'Like you, I am wondering how much he knows about Kukulcan and Santo Tomás...'

But he had not forgotten that the ancient box had its highly valued place right at the very heart of the Calendar Wheel. Without this precious gift from Kukulcan, the Wheel itself could not move forward.

'Please tell Father Delgado we will need it back soon,' he said, reminding his brother. We will need to get it back soon to open the Path of the Sacred Way...'

9

EARLY NEXT MORNING Itzamna made his way down to the church carrying the precious wooden box under his arm. Arriving at the paved stone square outside the church, he strode purposefully past the large colonial fountain in the centre of the forecourt. Then he headed towards the adjoining colonnade and walked through to the small enclosed garden at the back of the church. Pedro Delgado lived in a modest brick and stucco building, an annex with whitewashed walls, a tiled roof and a small verandah that nestled in behind the old colonial church. A leafy hibiscus tree with bright yellow flowers dominated the simple garden and random clusters of red and orange flowers had been planted in small clumps around its base.

Pedro Delgado was pottering around in the garden when Itzamna arrived. He looked up as he heard him approach.

'I was sorry to hear about your father...' he said, dusting off his hands. He had already heard the news.

'Thank you,' said Itzamna. 'He was old and frail. We all knew he couldn't last too long. But it's very sad when it actually happens....even when you're expecting it...'

Pedro invited him to sit down on one of the old wooden chairs that were resting on the verandah.

'I've got something I'd like to show you,' said Itzamna.

He placed the box carefully on the empty chair beside him.

'But first may I ask ...?

He hesitated, but then decided he'd raise the subject anyway.

'What have you heard about Kukulcan and Jesus's disciple Santo Tomás?

Is there any connection...? '

Pedro leaned back in his chair and paused for a moment, resting the palm of his hand against his chin. No-one had asked him about this for quite some time.

'There are many stories about Santo Tomás,' he said finally. 'There are so many stories, it's hard to know what to believe. Some people say that he came to the Americas soon after the crucifixion of Jesus. Some say he went first to southern India and set up a Christian church there, and then he came in a large wooden boat from India to Guatemala. There were excellent boat-builders in India at the time. It's possible, I suppose...'

'And Kukulcan..?'

'Well, the local people had different names for Santo Tomás. According to all the legends the Aztecs respected him as a man of peace. Some people say he is Quetzalcoatl in another guise, that in reality they are one and the same...'

'And the Mayan people...?'

'Well, as you know, the Mayan name for Quetzalcoatl is Kukulcan. I don't know if there is an exact connection. Why do you ask?'

'As you know, my father regarded himself as the senior local shaman,' said Itzamna. '...as the chosen custodian of the sacred Calendar Wheel...'

Pedro nodded silently. Everyone knew that Nachancan had been a respected shaman and a well-liked leader of his people. Some of the Mayan villagers may have switched their allegiance to the Christian Mission but they still held him in high regard, Pedro knew that for sure.

'He was widely admired by everyone around here,' said Pedro. He had known the old man for many years and sometimes they shared a few stories together in the market square. Pedro fully appreciated that his passing was an enormous loss to the Mayan community.

'But my father claimed something else as well,' said Itzamna. 'He told my brother he was the custodian for the secret teachings of Kukulcan, that he was keeping them safe until the right time came to talk about them openly. He said these teachings had been passed down through the shaman-line from the earliest

45

times. He said that Santo Tomás had left them as a gift for our people...'

Pedro looked doubtful and mildly sceptical. If there were secret teachings like that he certainly hadn't heard about them until now.

'Tell me more about these secret teachings... this gift from Santo Tomás' he said, probing a little deeper.

'Arana says the teachings speak of the Second Coming... that the world will change on the final day of the Calendar Wheel...'

Itzamna looked searchingly at Father Delgado. He felt sure he was someone he could trust, someone whose opinions he could value. He had begun to regard him almost like a second father since coming to services at the Mission. Now he had brought the box and the scroll for him to look at, so he could decide for himself.

'Here are the teachings, 'he said simply. 'They're in here. They're in this old box...'

He passed it across.

Pedro took the wooden box and examined its scarred and weather-worn surfaces, turning it around and looking at it from several different angles. Then he carefully eased back the lid. Inside he could see the scroll fragments, with their curious markings. The scroll itself looked very old and delicate, so delicate that for a brief moment he felt hesitant about even opening the box at all.

'Remarkable...' he said simply, after gazing at the fragments for quite some time. 'This is really very remarkable...'

Peering into the box he tried to decipher the writing, or at least determine what sort of script the text was written in. It looked very different from ancient Greek. He had transcribed copies of several of the earliest biblical texts while he was still at college, when he was studying theology in Barcelona, and this script looked completely different. The letters were very distinctive. They were more angular, more archaic.

46

He looked across at Itzamna with a puzzled look on his face. This really was an unusual discovery...

'I don't know,' he said finally. 'I really don't know what to make of it...'

Itzamna wondered if he should return the box to his brother and pretend he had never seen it. Then Pedro had an idea. Suddenly his face was beaming with enthusiasm.

'There is someone I can ask... someone who will know...'

He got up quickly from his chair, clutching the box tightly in his hands, holding it close as if cradling a precious relic.

'May I keep this for a while? There is someone I can ask... someone who will know for sure whether this is important or not...'

* * *

Two weeks later Pedro Delgado went down to the market square to meet the local bus as it came in from Panajachel on its daily visit. The expectant crowd had already begun to gather: a cluster of bronze-skinned men wearing bleached straw hats and carrying large woollen bags for the return journey, several happy, chattering girls all travelling together, a group of jovial women with their brightly coloured shawls and a clutch of happy playful children, together with a number of local onlookers and a few stray dogs in search of discarded food scraps.

As always, the distinctive red and yellow bus was late, but when it did arrive, screeching to a sudden halt in a cloud of dust, everyone inside was suddenly clambering to get out, carrying with them their bulging bags of vegetables and small goods, their wooden boxes of tools and appliances, their bundles of cut flowers. Their friends were there to greet them as well, and the weary driver, a short balding man with a bead of sweat across his brow, honked the horn of the old school bus once or twice for good measure. The arrival of the Panajachel bus was always a daily event in the village square, and definitely not to be missed.

Emerging from the crowd was a short, stocky man with a bushy black moustache and an elegant grey suit. He was carrying a valise and a smart new suitcase that had suffered several indignities during the journey. Looking down he brushed some dirt from his otherwise impeccable jacket, smoothed out the creases in his tie, and walked briskly across the square.

Pedro was there to meet him, holding out his hand to welcome him.

'Mario Burri... ?'

The two men hadn't met before but they had already spoken several times on the phone, the only effective form of international communication available in the remote Atitlán village.

'Welcome to Xocomil, it's good that you have got here at last!'

Pedro beamed a smile at him, but Mario Burri was in no mood to respond cheerfully. He was still recovering from the culture shock of travelling in a crowded, noisy American school bus along bumpy dirt roads, grinding up steep inclines and then weaving through small mountain valleys for well over an hour. It was very different from his research job in the Vatican archives, where everything ran like clockwork.

'It was fine up until Panajachel...' he said, trying hard to force a smile.

He was still feeling flustered and was looking forward to a cool drink, if one could be found.

'Let me help you with that...' said Pedro, reaching down for his suitcase.

The two men walked across the square, past the old colonial fountain and round to the back of the church.

'This will be your room, while you are here,' said Pedro, as they came in off the verandah. Placing the suitcase on the floor, he quickly adjusted the bedcovers which had slipped across to one side in the makeshift bedroom.

'It's a bit small, but we don't get many visitors, let alone biblical translators from Rome...!'

Mario Burri was starting to unwind.

He took off his jacket, loosened his tie and put the Italian newspaper he had been reading down next to the lamp on the small bedside table.

'I had a long flight followed by two very long bus rides, but I guess it's good to be here,' he said finally. 'Cardinal Ratzinger insisted I should get here as soon as possible...'

'Make yourself at home,' said Pedro, doing everything he could to be hospitable. I'll get you a cold drink, I'm sure you'd like one. Rest up for a while...we can talk later...'

He hurried away and returned a few minutes later with a glass of freshly squeezed fruit juice.

'Put your feet up and take it easy for a while. I'll show you the text later on, when you've had time to unwind...'

Later that afternoon the two men came out and sat together on the verandah. Mario Burri placed the wooden box beside him on the table and began talking excitedly about the discovery they had just made.

'You really wouldn't expect to come across something like this in Guatemala, of all places,' he said, sipping on the drink Pedro had brought out for him. 'Guatemala is the last place you'd think of, to find a biblical text of this antiquity...'

Pedro nodded as Mario continued.

'Obviously it will take some time for me to copy all the text fragments and translate them but I am sure that Cardinal Ratzinger will be very interested...'

'You think so?' said Pedro

'I do indeed.' said his guest. 'In fact, I am sure of it...'

Mario Burri looked across at his host with a mixed sense of pride and elation. Whether they knew it or not, they were about to make history together.

'I think we may have discovered the earliest biblical text that has yet been found,' he said, with a congratulatory smile breaking out across his face.

'I think we may have just discovered a scroll that actually dates back to the time of Jesus. A text written in the very language spoken by the Saviour himself...'

* * *

❧❦

Part Two

Flavia

❧❦

10

ON THIS PARTICULAR DAY James Highgate had come in to the *Herald* early, which meant earlier than ten in the morning. Papers and magazines lay strewn across his desk and there was all the usual sort of basic grind to attend to. Polishing off yet another article on star footballer David Beckham... Finding out more about the 'father's rights' campaigner dressed in a Batman suit who had recently scaled the walls of Buckingham Palace as part of his public protest... Digging deeper into rumours about Liz Hurley's love life... Writing some sort of gossipy piece on the income-and-fame list published by *Forbes Magazine* which made Jennifer Aniston the most celebrated woman on the planet, ahead of Madonna and Nicole Kidman.

Still, he couldn't complain. The *Brighton Herald* had come a long way since Jo Lansbury had come in as chief features editor. Until quite recently the paper had languished quietly in the grey monotony zone populated by so many regional newspapers. With stories on local p & c groups, produce and livestock news, political squabbles on the local council, the occasional ceramics exhibition and the annual fashion derby at Wellington Mall, the *Herald* had looked like all the others. Now all that had been swept aside. Jo herself was an energetic, early 40s, slightly dumpy but hugely energetic woman with vivid red hair cut in a straight line across a cheerful open face. Her eyes always twinkled and she was a joy to work for. She invariably spoke with energetic sweeps of the hand and was loud and direct. 'To hell with the conservatives,' she had proclaimed exuberantly on hearing the news that a gay Anglican had been appointed as a bishop in the United States. 'Let's stir things up a bit and shake the status quo. I'm all in favour of shifting the boundaries...'

James' best qualities included a willingness to listen and an ability to get his head down, do the work, and deliver on time. He was an efficient writer, competent rather than flashy but good at focusing on the sort of popular detail that the readers wanted. The girls at the *Herald* liked him too, especially Libby Rankin – who was the other main features writer – and curly haired, bubbly Rachael, who worked as the office receptionist. Now pushing 37, James was a well built attractive six-footer with a generous smile and bright blue eyes. He kept his hair short and tidy and wore close-fitting shirts and sporting jackets to convey as much of an athletic image as possible, although the truth was that this particular persona was beginning to fray a little around the edges. He still played occasional social tennis and kept up with a regular regimen of swimming twenty lengths in the local pool every Sunday afternoon. However his body was already showing a few tell-tale signs that the sweet blush of youth was over.

James liked wining and dining as far as his modest income from the *Herald* allowed, and now there were clear signs that he was putting on weight. His belt buckle had recently moved along another notch and he also noticed that a small balding patch had appeared on the back of his head. Nevertheless, he was fully willing and able to embrace the good life, whenever it presented itself. He was still young at heart and liked flirting without deep commitment. And although he had only been in two lasting relationships since graduating in journalism from Warwick College all those years ago, he felt certain that the right partner was out there somewhere and it was only a matter of time before they found each other. His mother, who had died last year, had been distant and remote, and he had never been close to his elderly father who was now in a nursing home in Bridport suffering from Parkinson's Disease. So, as an only child who had arrived late in his parent's life, there was little emotional comfort on the home front to build on. James believed that any sense of self-confidence he now possessed had arisen entirely by itself, like a mutation, probably out of sheer desperation. He was on his own now, and coming to Brighton as a journalist for the local newspaper was really a lucky break. James Highgate, feature writer...

They had now started calling it London by the sea, and in a way it was. Certainly, the signs of Brighton's provincial past still lingered along the narrow streets adjoining Grand Parade. There were the inevitable pockets of weather-worn bed & breakfasts, aging gift shops with sun-faded displays, and run-down grocery shops that closed too early in the afternoon. But up in the Lanes and North Lanes districts, with their funky coffee shops, wine bars, elegant eateries and avant-garde fashion boutiques, Brighton was definitely coming back to life. One of his favourites was a small restaurant called The Sandman, which nestled in a lane a short walk from Churchill Square. The food on offer had moved beyond nouvelle cuisine to something much more substantial but the presentation remained stylish and sophisticated. There were excellent, reasonably priced French and Australian merlots on the wine list and the decor was welcoming but understated. The semi-abstract flower and animal prints on the wall were in a soft European pastel style and were mounted in tasteful unpainted wooden frames. James didn't go in for chrome or techno so this was much more to his style – for him, an accessible expression of regional cosmopolitan taste. A single vivid flower in a fine-necked vase adorned each table. James often came here, alone or sometimes with Libby, to gather his thoughts over lunch and plan the stories he had to write during the next few days. He was here with Libby today.

Libby had a depth he admired, a serious and elusive quality that he could never quite put his finger on. She was tall and slim, and wore her straight dark brown hair in a pageboy style. Her face was finely sculpted and delicate, her eyes grey-blue and clear. James especially liked the way she held her wine glass, the way she lifted it carefully to her lips. There was an elegance in this that he hadn't noticed in other young women he knew. But although she was stylish in her own special way, Libby sometimes wore clothes that made her look rather austere – like today, for example, with her respectable navy skirt and her buttoned lace blouse...

Although she was still in her late twenties Libby often looked several years older. There was just a hint of the shy librarian about her, a distinct feeling of passion repressed. Libby came from a wealthy family in Wiltshire and had graduated with an arts degree from Oxford. She already had two stories published in a literary anthology and in her spare time was working on some longer prose pieces that could hopefully become a novella. 'My reflective pieces...' she called them. Sometimes James imagined her as a sort of modern day suffragette figure, as a person given to worthy social and philosophical causes, someone who could transcend the trivia and who was truly in touch with the bigger picture. In a word, she was smarter than him.

Libby had slotted into what Jo referred to as a journalist's niche and wrote most of the stories on wildlife and the environment. She also profiled the distinguished literary and political figures who passed through town from time to time....especially the notables and celebrities who attended university conferences or launches at the upmarket Black Crow bookshop.

From time to time James found to his surprise and occasional delight that the people he worked with intruded on his dreams. Rachael, who was busty and earthy, bobbed into his dreams every now and then, usually in a playful sort of way. And now, just two nights ago, James had had a dream in which he and Libby were playing tennis naked together. Far from being erotic, however, it was a nakedness shorn of passion and spontaneity. In the dream Libby had an ethereal beauty as if her body were fashioned from white marble. Her movements were fluid and poetic, her hair like liquid silk. The game itself had been intense and energetic, and yet the mood of the dream was clinical and detached. James remembered later that he had lost the game they were playing without even winning a point and that Libby had a surprisingly tricky serve that curled the ball across the court. Maybe that actually proved that she was smarter than him. James hadn't told Libby about the dream, and he wasn't about to tell her now.

'There's a book launch tonight at the Black Crow...,' said Libby, finishing her coffee and reaching inside her bag for the personally signed invitation. 'It's a new book by Jeremy Lansing....'

She paused for a moment and looked out into the street, distracted by someone passing whom she remembered from a recent social occasion.

'You know,' she continued. '...that political correspondent who does all those inside stories about Moslem fundamentalists for Channel Four. His new book is about subversive Moslem clerics in Iraq... Lansing says they're undermining George Bush's strategy for the new world order. It sounds interesting but I could use some company in case all the social chat gets too intense. I might find myself needing someone normal to talk to...'

Libby smiled sweetly across the table. No question, James was definitely more normal than Jeremy Lansing but also a lot more appealing. She definitely wanted him to be there.

'It starts at 6:30,' said Libby. 'Interested in coming...?'

James immediately pictured the scene: Libby making intelligent and insightful conversation with the glamorous and vociferous Jeremy Lansing. Then being swept to one side by Tom Hankley, the theatrical and effusive manager of the Black Crow, before being dragged off to meet a 'fascinating young novelist... who's already making his mark in the New York SoHo scene'. There would be endless rounds of mediocre wine, slim pencil-shaped sandwiches with indiscernible fillings, and the unstated promise of ravishing literary conversation into the early hours of the evening. James hated the pretensions of the Black Crow but he could see that Libby really wanted to go. He definitely wasn't in the mood – he would have to go home first to arrange a recording of the crucial Manchester United-Aston Villa match – but it looked like he was destined for the Black Crow. Something in Libby's questioning gaze had compelled him to agree.

'Sure...' he said, trying as hard as possible to mask his distinct lack of enthusiasm. 'I'll come over to your place around 6:15 ... it's only a short walk down to North Lanes.'

Libby packed her bag and got ready to go. James looked up sheepishly with a half grin on his face. He was trying for a moment to imagine her naked again, like in the dream, but his brain orchestrated a predictable murmur instead.

'I'll do my best to look interested in what Jeremy Lansing has to say...' he said.

'6:15 at your place...'

* * *

Although she was now mostly hidden within her dark green leather jacket, James noticed that Libby had changed into an apricot-pink blouse and was looking surprisingly glamorous. Her long flowing scarf looked great, too. Suddenly, in an instant, the librarian image had vanished. As they walked together down the hill from Finchley Square, Libby teasingly thrust her arm around him and drew him closer. 'Well, Mr Highgate,' she whispered softly in his ear, 'I have succeeded in enticing you down to the Black Crow. I'm sure you'll survive to tell the tale...'

The crowd was already spilling into the street from the Black Crow as James and Libby arrived. A few noisy and opinionated guests had entered into a heated discussion about the merits of the American occupation of Iraq and the response of Moslem clerics from neighbouring Iran. Meanwhile, another group of bystanders had begun loudly debating the political strategies associated with the world's crude oil market. Inside the Black

Crow bookshop a long queue of purchasers had already formed, eager to have the well known television celebrity Jeremy Lansing inscribe their copies with his inimitable personal flourish. Soon there were the predictable speeches, with Jeremy Lansing offering thanks for the opportunity to present *The Revolt of the Clerics* to the good people of Brighton and to everyone who appreciated the precarious nature of current world politics. This was followed, of course, by further rounds of mediocre wine and pencil-thin sandwiches. As anticipated, Libby soon found herself engaged in a detailed conversation with the celebrated author himself – details which, it was hoped, would soon find their way into the robust pages of the *Brighton Herald*.

Then, bustling through the burgeoning crowd, Tom Hankley descended on Libby and eased her away from Jeremy Lansing just as he was pausing at that very moment to draw breath. While Lansing himself was pondering whether all the major points in his publicity drive had been covered, Tom had already moved on to the prospect of next week's celebrity book-signing. 'Dearest Libby,' said Tom, sweeping her away from the celebrated guest in his most effusive and theatrical style, 'There's someone else here I'd love you to meet... a fascinating young novelist who's visiting Brighton for a few days and who's already making his mark in the New York SoHo scene...'

Overhearing the conversation, James knew then that he was truly prescient, that he had tapped a mysterious supernatural power that enabled him to foresee what would inevitably occur at literary gatherings like these. And as he continued to sip from his glass of mediocre wine and gingerly consume the pencil-thin sandwiches with indiscernible fillings presented on the plate of available offerings, he wondered how long his patience would last.

Fortunately Libby didn't want to stay too long at the Black Crow. Within a few minutes she had emerged through the bustling crowd, clutching two bottles of Moet under her arm. ' I managed to weasel myself away from that SoHo writer of Tom's – he was really pretentious – but Jeremy gave me these, courtesy of his generous publisher.' Libby beamed at James, stroking the bottles enthusiastically. 'Of course, he expects a substantial piece in the *Herald*, but I can write that tomorrow. Let's go back to my place and have a proper drink...'

This was a very different Libby Rankin from the more reserved and diffident colleague James worked with at the office. Right now she was positively bubbling with excitement, bursting with the possibilities of the moment. Clutching James once again to her side, Libby set off up the hill to her flat at Finchley Square.

'Do you like my new Tara Duncan print?' she enthused as they arrived, throwing her green leather jacket casually onto the sofa. 'I've been changing the look of everything... new sofa, new pot plants, great new exotic Moroccan cushions...'

James nestled down on the sofa, running his fingers across the richly textured fabric and taking it all in. Libby's flat looked classy and sophisticated, much more welcoming than his own modest abode. Soon small bowls containing asparagus, stuffed olives and exotic nuts had appeared on the table and then Libby thrust a tall fluted glass of bubbling champagne into his hand. 'Here's to us...,' she said enthusiastically, 'Here's to the moment...'

Libby dimmed the lights and put on the most recent Clannad album, one James hadn't heard. Soon a muted Celtic ambience was floating through the room. Libby looked radiant and mysterious, her hair backlit in a soft amber glow. Suddenly it seemed that time itself had evaporated into nothingness, that all the earlier events of the evening had fused into a hazy, distant memory.

In an instant Libby had slipped across and was sitting teasingly next to James on the sofa. Nestling beside him she took another sip of champagne from her glass and thrust her head back enticingly into the luxurious Moroccan cushions. James had never seen her looked so mysterious or alluring. Her cheeks reflected just the faintest soft hint of a warm and sensuous flush and he could see her eyes glistening in the muted light. Her glamorous apricot blouse fell in soft folds and lay enticingly open at the neck, revealing pearly-white skin. Suddenly Libby had transformed from a shy journalist into an exotic seductress.

She moved up closer beside him, stroking his hair before gently caressing his cheeks and feeling for his mouth with her lips. James could feel his pulse lifting as Libby pressed up against him. 'Here's to the moment,' she purred again in his ear, 'Here's to us...'

Now she became the complete enticer, kneeling in front of him, deftly unbuttoning her blouse and then letting it fall beside her on the carpet. Her skin glistened with a pearly softness. Her neat sculpted breasts were just as James had seen them in his dream, with the innocent pink nipples of a young girl.

James quickly unbuttoned his shirt, cast off his trousers in almost indecent haste, and let Libby slide on top of him, her warm skin merging into his, the soft form of her body seducing him through its intimacy. He allowed his searching hands to caress the inviting textures of her skin, gently exploring the curve of her back and feeling the pulsing warmth of her thighs. Now she was holding him and stroking him, making him firm before easing him gently inside her, gliding like the silence of a river. And the tide was quickening. James flowed and thrust and swam within her, like the dance of a summer ocean. Soon she was panting and writhing with delight, with all the sensual innocence of a newly discovered pleasure. Seizing all the sweet juice out of the precious, ecstatic moment....

11

BUT IT ALL PASSED QUICKLY BY, like yet another dream. Next day James looked up with an ironic smile on his lips as Libby slipped past him on the way to her desk, pretending not to notice him. They had agreed that this must remain their special secret, their special intimacy, and there was no way either of them would let their secret slip out. No way would they let themselves become the focus of cheap and tacky gossip in the office. On the surface at least, it was back to business. James could just imagine how Rachael would react, if she found out. It would be all over the office, with sniggerings, whispers and secret finger pointing. Jo would probably have something to say about it as well.

Not that Jo's emotional entanglements were without problems of their own. Until last month Jo had notched up three years living off and on with a Caribbean blues musician called Marley. But it was a relationship that was beginning to fizzle out, mostly through a lack of enthusiasm on her part. Admittedly, there were still little tugs and pulls that brought them together from time to time. Their friends still overlapped but their careers, specifically hers, were now heading in quite different directions. In a word, Jo was hoping to go somewhere while Marley was mostly going nowhere. Marley still hung around the *Herald* office from time to time, hoping, perhaps, for some of Jo's new-found success to rub off on him.

But even if Jo had gone cool on him James liked Marley a lot, and sometimes they went for drink together when they felt like a bit of soul-brother talk. On those occasions James and Marley would find themselves drinking far too many frothy lagers as they reflected on the good old times when the blues were the blues, and real reggae was the sort of reggae that came out of Kingston, Jamaica. Long before Robert Cray and UB40 and Simply Red, when you could pick out Robert Johnson and Muddy Waters and

Freddie King and Otis Rush and Bob Marley... before the blues and reggae had become more commercial. 'Hey, man,' Marley had told James the first time they got together in the White Hog Bar, '... D'ya know my full name? My mother named me Marley Hendrix Otis Tosh Wilson when I was born. She loved this music. She knew a thing or two...'

But as Marley was freely willing to admit, he and Jo had fallen on tough emotional times. Part of it had to do with what Jo described as his happy-go-lucky attitude to life in general. Like a true rasta-man Marley loved the odd reefer and could stay up all night, improvising and singing the blues with his friends:

Oh, have you ever met that funny Reefer Man, Reefer Man?
Have you ever met that funny Reefer Man, Reefer Man,
If he says he swam to China,
And he'll sell you South Carolina,
Then you know you talkin' to that Reefer Man...

Jo wanted something much more focused, something which actually headed somewhere. She had been a good freelance journalist for years, publishing articles on jazz and blues in the *Guardian* as well as contributing more general pieces to the weekend glossies. Now she had come to Brighton as the new features manager on the *Herald*. And while the paper didn't have a great pedigree, Jo believed she could make it change, make it happen, by breathing new life into its grey regional body. Marley had tagged along, of course, expecting all the while to get regular gigs with the blues bands that played from time to time in North Lanes. But the gigs were few and far between, and the calibre of the music fell well below Marley's hopes and expectations. So Marley and Jo had begun drifting apart. She lived by herself now. Usually when he called by the office, Jo would tell him either to get lost or to get a life, depending on her mood at the time.

On this particular day, the day after the unanticipated

seduction, Marley was hanging about near the entrance to the *Herald* just as James decided to pop out for a few minutes to get a coffee from Ziggi's.

'Wanna come up to Ziggi's for a break ?' James asked him as their eyes met. Ziggi's was one of their regular haunts. This coffee shop was much more zippy than the White Hog Bar and had bright orange, purple, red and yellow murals, vaguely in the wild pop art style of Keith Haring. A bit over the top, but the coffee was good. Marley nodded and they headed off towards the Lanes

'What do you think about dreams?' said James in a non-committal, pretending-to-be-only-vaguely interested sort of way, as they shuffled past a line of sun-faded gift shops. 'Do you think they ever give you a taste of what's going to happen next?'

'Dunno, man.' Marley was thinking about a particular blues riff that he was going to try out at his next gig.

'Well, see what you think about this,' said James, totally oblivious of the fact that Marley was only mildly interested in what he was saying at this particular moment. 'Two nights ago I had this dream about this woman I know. Like, I don't really know her, but I see her from time to time. And there is she is, popping up in my dream. And you know what..?'

Marley was still thinking about his guitar riff as James continued, caught up in his recollections.

'She was naked, and we started playing a game of tennis...'

'Who won?' asked Marley, feigning mild interest.

'She did, but that's not what I'm leading up to...'

'What are you leading up to?' said Marley, still with his mind on other things. He was thinking he might try shifting from A minor to F, come down hard on the bass string and then finish up either on G or A seventh.

'Well, last night I actually got seduced by the same woman. And she looked like a marble-skinned goddess in real life. Just like in the dream.'

'No shit,' said Marley. 'Was she good?'

'She was good…surprisingly good…'

'No shit,' said Marley, who hadn't scored any body contact with a marble-skinned goddess in quite some time.

They turned into Hitchcock Lane and started walking up the hill to Ziggi's.

Until now James hadn't been concentrating on anything much except his dream fantasies and his craving for a mid-morning coffee. But just beside the entrance to Caxton Hall, a poster caught his eye.

Secrets of the Inquisition: Exhibition Opening
Wednesday, 24 September, 8 p.m

Wednesday 24, 8 p.m. – that was tonight. An inside glimpse into the Inquisition. That was something different. Very different. Maybe a feature story with a bit of a devilish twist. James imagined a row of sinister, black-caped Inquisitors gathered together in a sombre medieval chamber, staring down an innocent waif before pronouncing sentence and then sending the hapless victim off to be executed. All a bit gruesome…

He read on, scanning the fine print..

An exhibition of medieval artifacts and documents
from the Age of Cruelty and Torture.
Address by Giuseppe Martino, archivist from the Vatican…

James was intrigued, morbidly fascinated. It sounded grimly appealing in a perverse sort of way and he felt sure there would be a story in it. It was quite unexpected for something like this to surface in Brighton but then, in its own day, the Inquisition had reached out all over Europe. He remembered seeing some macabre woodcuts of the witchcraft persecutions in an old history book.

James called out to Marley who was already disappearing way

off in the distance. 'Hey, Marley,' said James. '... take a look at this.' Marley shuffled back to where James was standing, outside the entrance to Caxton Hall. Together they read over the details. Marley was fascinated too, and looked on as James jotted down a few hasty notes in his diary. When James was finished with his notes they went on up to Ziggi's where the lure of a good, flavoursome coffee was sure to hit the spot.

'Those Inquisitors... jeez man, they were evil dudes,' said Marley reflectively as the capuccino froth made a white line along his thick dark lips.

James grunted in agreement. He had always been fascinated by the power of the medieval Church and its campaign to root out heretics and dissenters, even though his own life lacked any sense of drama or intrigue on that sort of level. It was like a whole other world, far removed from his daily routine of tabloid stories and celebrity gossip.

'Those guys went to their deaths just for believing something different,' said Marley, continuing his line of thought. Most days he felt like a total outsider too, especially when Jo got into one of her tyrannical outbursts. In medieval times you paid with your life if you didn't toe the line. But that was then and now was now. At least the coffee was good...

They agreed to check out the exhibition and meet outside Caxton Hall just before eight. Marley was already beginning to think of the lyrics for a new song called *Heretic Blues* :

When you turn your world against me babe,
I feel so cold and all alone.
I'm a stranger and a prisoner,
And I'm trapped here on my own.
You cast me into darkness babe,
I got them ole heretic blues again...

65

12

BY THE TIME THEY GOT TO Caxton Hall a large crowd had already gathered. Thunder clouds were rumbling overhead and heavy intermittent rain had begun to fall, streaking dark stains across the red bricks of the austere Victorian building. But that hadn't kept the visitors away. People were pouring in all directions through the main exhibition area, soaking up all the background information on the grimly fascinating items on show. Marley called James across to look at a display which included items of torture that had been used by the Inquisitors in southern France and Italy : thumbscrews, leg-screws, pincers, the so-called 'heating chair', cleavers, a metal implement known as the 'choking-pear', brands used to burn the skin, smouldering irons inserted between the buttocks...

'Animals...,' said Marley, hissing through his teeth. 'Those Inquisitors were bloody animals...'

James nodded in agreement. He was already scribbling down notes for his piece in the *Herald*. Some of the victims accused by the Inquisition of practising witchcraft had been tortured using a hateful method known as *strappado*. Their arms were tied behind their backs and they were then hoisted into the air using a pulley. Sometimes extra weights were attached to their legs, wrenching their shoulders from their sockets. There was an even more horrifying variation known as *squassation*, described in a historical document dating back to 1692. Here the hoisted captives were raised above the ground and then suddenly dropped from a considerable height while still remaining suspended by the rope. In this way their feet remained hovering just above the ground. The greater the height from which they were dropped, the greater the pain. Many accused witches and heretics – innocent or otherwise – had died from the effects of brutal torture like this.

James couldn't believe that the Inquisitors – who in theory, at least, were God-fearing Christians – could inflict such sadistic harm on their fellow human beings. It beggared belief and was totally beyond his comprehension. The whole period of the witchcraft and heresy persecutions was totally unlike anything he had ever encountered before.

There was an account of the Italian philosopher and former Dominican friar, Giordano Bruno, who had defied Church doctrine by referring to the stars in the night sky as the sons of God, and who claimed that God was present in every grain of sand. For holding these views Giordano Bruno had been burnt at the stake.

Also on display was an incriminating document, exacted after torture, which had been signed in blood by a Roman Catholic priest named Father Louis Gaufridi. It turned out that some nuns in a convent in Aix-en-Provence had accused Gaufridi of entering into a pact with the Devil. The nuns claimed that because of Gaufridi's evil pact they in turn had become possessed by demonic forces. Gaufridi was taken away and tortured and the Inquisitors were able to produce a confession from him which they claimed had been 'witnessed' by a number of demons including Ashtaroth, Asmodeus, and Beelzebub. In April 1611, Gaufridi was found guilty of practising demonic magic and sorcery. He was sentenced to death and then burnt alive. This happened just a few years after the execution of Giordano Bruno. By the end of the seventeenth century over 100,000 people had been accused of witchcraft and executed by the Inquisition. Many of them were innocent women who had been stripped naked by the Inquisitors to see if their bodies revealed signs of 'the Devil's mark'.

It was all too much to comprehend. Even putting aside the grisly facts themselves, James wondered why an exhibition like this had even been assembled. Why would the Catholic Church want to air some of its dirtiest linen? What was the reason for bringing all this horror and persecution out into the open? How could the Church hope to gain from the media publicity that would flow from an exhibition like this? After all, the secret dealings of the Inquisition had been hidden away for centuries behind closed doors in the Vatican. Now it was all out in the open for the first time. So why was this happening in Brighton? James would later discover that Father Evan Rotheram, Dean of the local Catholic seminary in Brighton, was a friend of Giuseppe Martino – they had studied theology in Edinburgh together – and this had helped Brighton get the jump on London. The exhibition was scheduled to move from Brighton to London for a much larger media launch in three months' time.

As a few last-minute rain-drenched arrivals swept into Caxton Hall there was an announcement that visitors should all make their way to the seated area near the podium, where Giuseppe Martino would give his presentation.

This will be interesting, thought James to himself. Was the Church now about to bare its soul and come clean about all this scandal? He called across to Marley to join him. Together they scrambled down towards the front, where they could be sure of a good seat.

They managed to find two vacant seats just three rows back from the podium, next to an austere looking, well-dressed, middle-aged woman with an aquiline profile and an intense stare. She looked determined to discover the secrets of the Inquisition at any cost. James wondered whether she had inquisitorial aspirations of her own. She was accompanied by a sombre -looking man who seemed to be her husband, and who had obviously been dragged along to the event against his best wishes. On his left, Marley found himself hemmed in uncomfortably against a balding, overweight man in a leather jacket who had come to the exhibition with his two teenage sons. They were loudly disputing the most gory items on display amidst the disapproving glances of others nearby.

'Put a sock in it, will yer,' said the leather-jacketed father, elbowing the son closest to him. '...he's just coming on to speak...'

The son quietened down as Father Evan Rotheram offered a brief introduction and invited his distinguished visitor to begin his address. Giuseppe Martino then moved up to the microphone which was mounted on the podium. He was a tall, elegant man in his fifties and had something of the air of a professional diplomat. Olive-skinned, with an authoritative, chiselled face and an impeccable pencil-line moustache, he looked ideally suited to guard the Index of Forbidden Books in the Vatican Library.

'Ladies and Gentleman,' he began, revealing a cultured Italian accent. 'It is some years since I have been in Britain, although I was here in my student days – in Edinburgh, actually – with my good friend Evan Rotherham, who is now Dean of the Roman Catholic Seminary here in Brighton.'

Pausing for a moment to cast his gaze across the gathering of seated guests, he took a brief sip from a glass of water and then looked down at his notes. James instinctively continued scribbling notes of his own but then suddenly remembered that his pocket tape-recorder was powerful enough to capture some choice quotes above the murmurings of the crowd. Reaching quickly into his pocket he grabbed his recorder, bumped up the volume and switched it on. The distinguished Vatican visitor was already continuing with his address.

'This exhibition reflects the new spirit of openness in the Roman Catholic Church. Unfortunately there have been several dark episodes in our past, especially during medieval times. We are not proud of them, but they must be addressed. Our Holy Father, as many of you will know, has asked God's forgiveness for these transgressions... forgiveness for sins committed by influential members of the Church. The tragic, misplaced persecutions of the Inquisition — examples of which you can now see for yourself in this exhibition — are foremost on the list of such evil deeds....'

Signor Martino now went on to explain his own role in the proceedings.

'So why is that I have come here to Brighton?' he asked rhetorically, gesturing in the air to make his point. 'Well, I am a professional archivist... that is my profession... I work in the Vatican for Cardinal Joseph Ratzinger who has responsibility for what is known – maybe rather too dramatically – as the Index of Forbidden Books. These include the secrets of the Inquisition... secrets which for many centuries have been locked away in our vaults. But since 1998, when Cardinal Ratzinger received authority from the Holy Father and announced a new spirit of openness and accountability in relation to these secret archives, the vaults in the Vatican have been opened to serious theological scholarship. The vaults have been opened so we can gain a new understanding of what has happened in the past. And this exhibition is also part of that process, a way of addressing the misplaced deeds and tragedies of former times. A way that helps us move forward into the future with a new spirit of hope and understanding....'

The well-dressed lady with the aquiline profile nodded in silent approval beside her sombre husband. Meanwhile the two teenage sons seated close to Marley had started fidgeting. The leather-coated father nudged the boy next to him with a swift thrust of the elbow and an only partially muffled curse. An uneasy silence then settled over the third row of seated guests as Giuseppe Martino drew his presentation to a close.

'So, ladies and gentleman, welcome to this exhibition.... We have called it "Secrets of the Inquisition". Maybe there are some questions you would like to ask...?'

A tall elderly man in a tweed jacket, who had been sitting a short distance away from James and Marley, now rose to his feet.

'How do we know that all the secrets of the Inquisition are really out in the open?' he asked aggressively. 'The Church has covered up its dark secrets for centuries. Why should we trust

70

you now?'

'Well,' replied Signor Martino, adopting a calm and diplomatic manner, '...as I have said, there is now a new spirit of openness... a deliberate and intentional policy of openness. We are addressing what happened in the past, so we can build a more positive future...'

'Don't think you can fob me off with platitudes!' growled the elderly man angrily as he gestured in the air with his carved walking stick. 'Thousands of innocent people went to their deaths because of the likes of you! Thousands and thousands of innocent victims, all in the name of Church power...'

He sat down, still bristling.

Someone else then asked a question about the mystical leanings of Giordano Bruno but Signor Martino already sensed that any further questions might soon lead him into more difficult territory. Clearly it was time to bring an end to all this. He quickly withdrew and allowed Father Rotheram to replace him on the podium.

'Please spend some time and have a good look at the exhibits on show,' said Father Rotheram, by way of bringing this part of the evening to a close. Never one to vigorously contest the fine points of Church politics, he had been surprised by the hostility of the opening question and felt uneasy filling the vacuum created by his departed guest. 'There will be drinks and snacks later, if you want to stay on afterwards ...'

The visitors spilled out once again through the exhibition area, some eager to make further discoveries, others keen to depart. The aquiline woman and her reluctant husband were now closely examining a historical text on the persecution of Cathar heretics in the region around Toulouse, but the leather-jacketed man and his two teenage sons had seen enough and decided to head off into the rain. Meanwhile Marley had noticed a half-open door leading to a dimly lit room at the back of the hall and he wondered if any further secrets lay in there.

71

Venturing in, he noticed a large display cabinet with a variety of additional thumbscrews and scalding irons, and what looked like dismantled sections of a torture rack.

He signalled silently for James to join him.

They were kneeling on the floor behind the cabinet when Father Evan Rotheram and Signor Martino burst into the room. Martino's suave and diplomatic manner had completely deserted him. He was angry. *Very* angry.

'No more questions from the floor...no more questions like that!' said Martino, emphatically. 'It's all too risky. It can get out of hand. Any more questions like that and it will undermine the whole purpose of this exercise...'

'Questions like what?' asked Rotheram, appreciating that his guest was not only agitated but also profoundly embarrassed. He was deeply grateful that Martino had gone out on a limb to put Brighton ahead of London and he was keen to calm the waters.

'Questions which challenge our honesty,' said Martino through gritted teeth. 'Questions which ask why we are doing all this...'

He lowered his voice and continued.

'There are some bigger issues at stake...'

'Bigger issues...?' asked Rotheram.

'Bigger issues,' said Martino, reinforcing his point.

Sensing further revelations, James quickly reached into his jacket pocket and switched on his tape recorder. He and Marley were still low down on the floor, well out of view.

'It's true that most of the secrets from the Vatican archive are now out in the open,' said Martino emphatically. 'But not all of them... There are some new developments. Recent developments... In Guatemala...'

'In Guatemala? What does Guatemala have to do with the Inquisition and Church doctrine?' asked Rotheram. He was genuinely perplexed, unable to make the connection.

Martino paused for a moment to recover his composure. He was still tense and on edge.

'They've found a new biblical text, an early text. It's in Aramaic, the language spoken by Jesus. It's probably earlier than the four main gospels... it may even be older than the Gospel of Thomas. I've discussed it with Cardinal Ratzinger and he wants it all kept under wraps until we can decipher it further.'

'Why is it so important?,' asked Rotheram, '...and what's the connection with Guatemala ? Guatemala's a long way from the Holy Land...'

'That's true,' said Martino. 'But the disciples travelled widely in the first century. We know that Thomas Didymos went to India. It now looks likely that he went to Central America as well. Soon after the crucifixion, spreading the word...'

'That's amazing,' said Rotheram. 'Does anyone else know about it?'

'Only a few scholars,' replied Martino. '... and Ratzinger has them all under his thumb. He has to, because it's political dynamite. It's a new version of Revelations....'

He paused to make his point more decisively.

'It actually goes beyond Revelations. It rewrites the Second Coming...'

'So, where's the manuscript now?' asked Rotherham nervously. 'Who's examining it?' He was fascinated by news of the important discovery.

'It's still in Guatemala, in the Xocomil church near Lake Atitlán. A priest named Pedro Delgado actually discovered it. He's been working with the Indians for years. I've sent Mario Burri over to look at it in detail. He's a specialist in Aramaic. It'll take him a while to review the complete text. I've asked for a preliminary report by the end of November. If necessary we'll arrange for the text to be sent to the Vatican, but that's easier said than done. The text's in bad shape. It could easily crumble and break up...'

Looking up cautiously, James watched the two men leave the room, deep in conversation. Rotheram seemed to be hanging on every word. No doubt about it, thought James, the old man with the walking stick had a valid point. Why trust the archivist from the Vatican? He had admitted as much himself. There were still secrets, after all...

Later, as guests gathered for drinks, James noticed that Signor Martino and Father Rotheram had allowed themselves to be surrounded by a harmless gathering of enthusiastic elderly women, well out of range from any barbs or potentially embarrassing questions. Amidst the bustle James could also pick out the elderly man with the walking stick... the man who had caused all the commotion.

'Hi Marley, what are you doing here?' asked a voice from behind as he felt a tug on his sleeve.

He swung round to see who it was.

'Flavia...! how'ya doing man?,' said Marley enthusiastically. Everyone was "man" to him. He was a hip rasta-bluesman, after all, and there was a certain image to keep up, even if gigs in North Lanes were few and far between.

'Fine. I've been getting into Bessie Smith and Nina Simone lately...'

'That's great. *Great.*' said Marley. He loved those 'blues wimmin' too. Especially the feisty ones...

Flavia looked as beautiful as ever...tall and slim, her long auburn hair sweeping elegantly over her shoulders. She had hazel eyes, Marley's favourite. He fancied her a lot, but she always seemed out of reach on a social level. Exotic. Mysterious. Like some sort of inaccessible goddess. At least they were both interested in the blues and could talk about that...at least they had that much in common...

'Meet my friend, James...,' said Marley, pulling James into view. 'He's a journo. Works at the *Herald*. With Jo. Feature stories, all the goss, that sort of stuff. He can tell you himself...'

She held out her hand, delicately balancing a glass of white wine in the other.

'Flavia Timmins...'

'Pleased to meet you. James... James Highgate. Like Marley said, I write features for the *Herald*. We're just nosing around...'

Flavia looked at him searchingly, as if mentally checking his credentials.

'You know each other from way back?' asked James nonchalantly. He was suddenly finding words difficult to come by and had become completely and utterly distracted by Flavia's exotic beauty. It was really amazing, sometimes, the contacts Marley had. The hidden life of the rasta man...

'I sometimes go to North Lanes to hear the new bands,' said Flavia, 'That's where I met Marley. I really like the women blues singers. Wish I could sing like them! But I can't, unfortunately...'

She flashed a quick smile. A dazzling row of pure white teeth. Searching, exotic hazel eyes. Coffee-olive skin. Maybe a hint of Latin blood there somewhere. James was impressed.

'What's the connection with heretics and persecutions?' he asked.

'I'm here with my uncle. He's fascinated by all these things. Thinks he was a persecuted Cathar in a past life. He's quite passionate about it. Don't get me wrong, I'm interested too. But it's a mission for him...'

She indicated across the room towards the elderly man with the carved walking stick.

'That's him, over there. The man who asked the tricky question! My dear Uncle Conrad....Would you like to come across and meet him?'

She smiled again. An elusive and mysterious smile. James was transfixed.

'Sure...' he said, as fleeting glimpses of naked dream women swam once again through his memory. What was it with some of these beautiful young women? What was it about their elusive and enticing natures? That special ability to be seductive and alluring without anything tangible or specific being expressed? Was it the body language...or just the look? She reminded him a little of Penelope Cruz, but she was taller and more willowy. He and Marley followed Flavia as she glided elegantly through the crowd.

'Uncle, this is Marley... and this is James...' she said as she introduced them.

'Conrad Elkington,' he responded, shaking their hands in turn. 'Delighted to meet you...'

He was much taller than he had appeared from where James and Marley were sitting. Bright- eyed and intense, with clear pink skin and a mane of thick white hair, he was a man in his late seventies, perhaps even his early eighties. But while Flavia definitely had some sort of Latin connection, he was very definitely English. Tweed jacket English. His voice had the cultured tone of a man steeped in academic learning. Perhaps he was a retired university professor? Or maybe just an eccentric aristocrat? He leaned slightly to one side, his weight supported by an elaborately carved walking stick. James noticed that it had some unusual symbols engraved on it. Maybe he'd ask about those later.

'Your question caused a bit of a stir,' said James with a grin on his face. He liked the old man immediately. There was something authoritative in the way he had stood his ground as he confronted the Vatican archivist. Something deeply impressive about the way he was willing to cut to the chase. He was obviously willing to speak his mind.

'These issues matter a lot to me,' he replied. 'They are big issues, issues that affect what we are told and what we come to believe...'

James nodded knowingly although he was actually unsure about the exact point Flavia's uncle was making. It sounded profound without being specific. For the moment James remained silent, hoping he would elaborate further.

'Tell them about the heretics, your obsession with heretics,' said Flavia, looking teasingly at her uncle.

'Well, Flavia's quite right,' he said. 'I am somewhat obsessed, if that's the right word. Obsessed with the nature of heresy and spiritual belief. I guess I have a tendency to side with the underdog and support the outsider. For centuries the Church has been telling us what to believe, and denying all forms of dissent. These persecutions, these tortures inflicted by the Inquisition, are a potent reminder of that...'

He motioned towards the exhibits, steadying himself at the same time on his trusted walking stick. No doubt about it, thought James, Flavia's Uncle Conrad was a man of strong convictions.

'And it's still going on,' he continued. 'The Inquisition has simply changed its name. Now they call it the Congregation of the Doctrine of the Faith, which in a way sounds quite harmless. But it's still the same old Inquisition in a new guise, even if they don't actually burn people at the stake any more. Cardinal Ratzinger's the man in charge at the Vatican. And Giuseppe Martino is just his PR man. They're doing everything they can to change their image...'

James thought maybe it was time to change the subject, at least for now. Marley was getting that glazed look in his eyes. Maybe he and Marley – and Flavia if she wanted to come – could head off to a pub or a wine bar for a quick drink. He could catch up with Uncle Conrad later.

'I'm working on a piece for the *Herald*,' said James, reaching into his pocket for one of his last dog-eared business cards. 'If it's all right with you, I'd like to do an interview with you for my story. Some time soon if that's convenient...'

'Sure,' said Conrad Elkington.' Come out and see me. We're

only a few miles away in the country, on one of the minor roads between here and Lewes. It's a pleasant enough drive. Flavia will give you the details of the best way to come. Ring first to make a time...'

He reached into his tweed jacket for a card of his own. The details were printed in simple embossed letters. James glanced quickly at it as he put it into his pocket:

Sir Conrad Elkington
Alpha and Omega
Castle Wilmington
Firle Grove, Sussex

The phone details were there too, in small black numerals, bottom right.

'Thanks,' he said, 'I'll ring and make a time to come out and see you...'

Flavia, meanwhile, had caught his eye. Then she looked across to Marley, whose interest in heretics was fading fast. Somehow Marley had tuned in to James' thoughts and body language which suggested that a social drink would be a nice idea.

'James and I are heading off to the White Hog after this ...' said Marley. 'Want to come for a drink and a bit of a chat? There's some good live music later on...'

'I'll drive Uncle Conrad home first,' she said, as he nodded approvingly. 'And then I'll come back to the White Hog...'

She gave him a cheeky smile.

'I won't be too long...'

13

GATHERING THEIR JACKET COLLARS up close to stay warm, James and Marley headed out into the stormy night. Rain splattered across the pavement as they hurried along, the streetlights casting hazy reflections on the cobblestone surfaces. The weather was closing in, but the night was still young.

It was only a short walk to the White Hog. According to Marley an acoustic folk-blues band called Mojo would be on later in the evening. They not only had a female lead singer but also a female lead guitarist as well. The guitarist, whose name was Jacki, played dazzling slide-guitar blues on a gleaming metal dobro. She had shaved her head almost entirely, leaving just a single tuft which she had dyed bright crimson. She also had a fantastic Celtic tattoo which went right around her arm. Marley thought she was hot. Flavia would probably be impressed too.

'Flavia's pretty amazing,' said James as they shuffled up the hill towards Churchill Square. 'How do you get to meet exotic women like her?'

'By playin' de blues, man,' said Marley, deftly kicking a discarded beer bottle to one side with his foot as they walked along. 'Hot wimmin, dey just loves de blues...'

Inside the White Hog a noisy group of beer-sodden soccer supporters had gathered to watch highlights of the Chelsea-Arsenal match but there was still a quiet corner away from the bar. Marley shuffled over to claim a table as James ordered a round of drinks. The usual. Two light ales to kick things off...

James was interested to find out more about Flavia, before she arrived.

Like what did she do, what were her interests, was she available, and was Marley chasing after her?

'No, man,' said Marley ruefully. 'I really like her, I really fancy her, but – hey, man – she's out of reach. She's a different sort of person...'

'Different in what way?'

'She's kinda mystical,' said Marley. 'She's different... Me, I'm more down-to-earth. Basic. She's more like a goddess. She's up there. Way up there...'

James sipped on his drink. Marley was getting reflective.

'I'm still hankering after Jo, man' said Marley, curling his lips across the top of his glass. 'Like, she kicked me out, but in here she's still my woman.'

He thumped his chest for effect.

'I like someone I can really hold onto if you get what I'm sayin'. Deep down I'm a rasta man. And like every rasta man, I fancy a big rasta woman...'

He smiled lustily.

James could easily imagine it. Rasta man and big rasta woman, getting it on. Hot love, huge passion. Jo wasn't black but she was definitely a soul-sister and she was very well-endowed. Now it was all falling apart between them. Maybe Jo would relent and take him back.

'Tell me more about Flavia,' he said, changing the subject. 'What's her background? What sort of work does she do?'

'Don't know that much about her', said Marley. 'She told me once that her grandmother was Spanish but apart from that she's a home-grown thoroughbred, if you get my meaning. Both parents died in a car accident two years ago... really tragic. I think she works as a linguist and translator some of the time, mostly here in Brighton. But she also spends quite a bit of time with Uncle Conrad and his wife up at the castle. They have some sort of magical research group going on up there. No idea what they actually do. Dunno anything else, man, I'm not really into it. Anyway, you can ask her yourself. Here she comes...'

Flavia was sweeping towards them past the bar, in the masterful, poetic way she had made her own. Gliding like a goddess past the unruly soccer supporters, she sat down next to

James.

'Fancy a drink?' he asked.

'Chardonnay would be nice,' she said, 'Crisp and cold, with a chunk of ice...'

James came back with her chilled glass of white wine.

'What happens in the magic castle?' he asked, changing tack.

'Has Marley been talking again behind my back? ' said Flavia. She glared across at Marley, pretending to be offended.

'Not really. He was just filling me in on Uncle Conrad's unusual interests.'

James flashed an ironic smile of his own. He liked finding out about people. Especially the sorts of things they did in private. That was the main attraction of journalism for him, after all. In his more honest moments he had to admit he was basically a bit of a voyeur.

'He has a magical research group, called Alpha and Omega. It's a small group. Friends...and other people who get invited. We meet at the castle. You only get to come if you're invited. Uncle Conrad has to approve...'

She took a sip from her glass.

'We study all the magical arts. *Real* magic. Magic that's gets into your soul and lifts your spirits...'

She suddenly sounded more formal and mysterious, as if she was revealing part of a precious secret.

'Native shamanism, Kabbalah, alchemy... a little bit of ritual. All that sort of thing...'

She put down her glass, as if getting ready to change the subject.

'It's all above board, though, 'she added. 'Nothing kinky or evil...'

James didn't know anything much about magic except for the occasional tabloid stories on witchcraft that appeared in the *Herald* from time to time. Fertility cults in the Sussex downs, naked women dancing around bonfires, strange incantations....

the sorts of stories that appealed to Sunday magazine readers. As for native shamanism, Kabbalah and alchemy – he simply had no idea what she was talking about. Even so, he wasn't ready to abandon the discussion just yet.

'Is it a real castle?' he asked, drawing the conversation down to a more basic level. 'I guess I'll get to see it soon. Your Uncle Conrad said I can come out and interview him for the *Herald*. In fact, you're supposed to tell me how to get there...'

'It actually is a real castle,' said Flavia crisply,'although it's not very big. Jacobite, built in the 1620s. It belonged to Lord Polegate, who's an ancestor of Uncle Conrad's. It's been in the Elkington family since 1790. Uncle Conrad and my father were brothers...'

'Were?' asked James.

'Mummy and daddy were killed in a car accident two years ago,' said Flavia. 'but I'd rather not go into that...'

Turning away from James she glanced across at Marley, who had started drumming his fingers on the table.

'When's the band coming on?' She asked, changing the drift of the conversation. 'Who are the singers...?'

'They're called Mojo', said Marley enthusiastically, 'and they're on in about ten minutes. Great female lead singer. Don't know her name. Sensational lady blues guitarist called Jacki, who has tattoos and a bright red tuft sticking up in the middle of her head...'

Flavia smiled.

'Sounds great!'

James sensed that maybe it was time to leave, that maybe he was beginning to overstay his welcome.

Flavia looked up as he gathered his jacket and got ready to go. She suddenly looked cool and just a little distant.

'Nice to meet you,' she said, extending her hand as if a formal interview had just come to an end. 'I'll draw a little a map showing how to drive up to Uncle Conrad's, and I'll drop it in to you at the *Herald*...'

14

WHEN JAMES got into the *Herald* next morning a small neat handwritten envelope was waiting for him at reception. Rachael smiled cheekily and handed it to him as he breezed past.

'A very nice young lady left this for you,' she said provocatively. 'Maybe it's a special invitation...'

James knew exactly what it was but he wasn't about to explain that to Rachael.

'Meeting in my office, soon as you can...' called Jo as he finally made it to his office. It was the usual Thursday morning gathering of the troops. Time to plan the main feature stories for the coming week.

Jo was uptight, James could tell.

'Saw Marley last night,' he said casually as he placed his coffee mug beside a cluster of news files. 'He sends his regards...'

'Great,' said Jo. 'That's the last thing I need to hear right now...'

Libby came in and sat down across the table and smiled her secret smile. They still had their secret, didn't they...

'Hi there' said James, giving nothing away. Business as usual.

Jo's secretary Val was also there, getting ready to take down notes from the meeting.

Jo was wearing her heavy-rimmed purple glasses, a garish medallion on a bulky golden chain and the mauve and green jacket she usually wore only to jazz club gatherings. She was also wearing tight yellow slacks, striped brown and white socks, and pale sky-blue shoes to match her bright red hair. A colour combination like that spelled trouble.

'I need a big story for Sunday,' she said, getting straight to the point.

'A three-page article that I can stretch across the main feature pages. Everything's looking very ordinary at the moment. In a word, without a decent feature story the weekend edition is stuffed...'

She took a quick swig of black coffee and rustled in her bag for her notepad.

'So what can you give me for Sunday?' she said, looking up at them from her half-opened bag. 'Something unusual, something topical, something quick. Something that's not just Posh and Becks, Fergie or Prince William. Something that the other papers won't be carrying....'

She looked across the table at Libby. Dependable Libby. Libby usually had something meaty and well-researched coming along.

'New international conference on the Kyoto Protocol... Japanese whaling in the Antarctic...President Bush still intent on mining for oil in Alaska...'

Libby scanned down her list as Jo tried desperately to stifle a yawn.

'A plague of badgers in the hills behind Eastbourne...no, just kidding. Sorry, nothing very interesting to report at the moment.'

'James...?'

'How about the dark secrets of the Inquisition?' said James. 'Instruments of torture, death and destruction. The Church finally comes clean about the scandals of the Middle Ages. An exhibition on heretics and the Inquisition opened in Brighton last night...I had a good look.'

James felt pleased with himself.

'Sounds fascinating,' said Jo. 'Any personalities to flesh out the story...? Interviews...? Profiles...?'

'I can profile the Vatican spokesman,' said James. 'He's in charge of something rather mysterious known as the Index of Forbidden Books. And I can also get an interview with a local personality who has strong views about heretics and persecution. His name is Sir Conrad Elkington and he lives in a castle...'

It was all too good to be true.

'Let's go with that,' she said abruptly.

Crisis averted.

* * *

'Looks like you scored a coup,' said Libby after the meeting. She was feeling a little envious and also rather surprised. It wasn't like James to dart off on a tangent like this. Celebrities and soccer personalities were more his specialty. She stood beside his desk looking sheepish and vulnerable.

James was trying hard not to gloat.

'Have to admit it was all a bit of a surprise...' he said finally, leaning back and folding his arms behind his head. 'I saw a notice that the exhibition was on. Marley and I went to the opening last night at Caxton Hall. There's all sorts of gruesome stuff in there...'

Libby looked impressed. She obviously wanted to hear more.

'Let's go up to Ziggi's for a coffee after work,' said James. 'I'll fill you in on all the details...'

Later they took the short stroll to Ziggi's. When they were out of view of the office Libby gave him a friendly kiss and put her arm around him. She was still bathed in the warm glow of their special intimacy two nights ago.

They sat at a table in the corner, looking out at the street, sipping their coffees. The cappucino foam was especially spectacular today and the waitress had sprayed a thick layer of fine cocoa across the top.

James told her in detail all about the exhibits at Caxton Hall... about the extraordinary range of scalding irons and torture implements, the presentation by the Vatican archivist Giuseppe Martino, and the chance meeting with Sir Conrad Elkington, whose provocative question about the true motives of the Church had clearly unnerved the distinguished guest.

Libby agreed that it all sounded really interesting, She wished she had been there.

She still had her arm around him when a striking young woman in an elegant full-length coat swept by. Looking into Ziggi's by chance, she caught James' eye. As her long auburn hair floated behind her, she smiled and waved without stopping.

'Who's that?' asked Libby as the young woman disappeared from view.

'That's Flavia Timmins' said James. 'She's Sir Conrad's niece. She was at the exhibition too...'

15

JAMES THOUGHT ABOUT FLAVIA for some time afterwards. She seemed to be sending him mixed messages. He thought she'd been rather cool and formal as he was leaving the White Hog but now the very next day here she was beaming a warm smile at him! James had to admit that he didn't always read women very well. Anyway, she must have decided that he was all right after all...

Early on Friday morning he phoned the castle and got Sir Conrad on the line. Within a few minutes the visit was arranged. They could meet at the castle at two that afternoon. That would be fine, thought James to himself, but he would have to get on with the story very quickly when he got back, in order to get it in to Jo in time. One definite plus, though, was that he could take the Morgan for a spin in the country. He hadn't done that for quite a while...

James' dark blue open-top Morgan sports car was his one indulgence. He'd had it for three years; it had been purchased largely through money he'd inherited when his mother died. It had traditional wire-spoke wheels, gleaming hubcaps, and black upholstery. It was already ten years old when he got it, so it was showing some signs of wear. Nevertheless it was a real thoroughbred. And it was so well made – a genuinely hand-crafted machine – and it would probably last for another fifty years. He liked the solid wooden trim and the authentic detailing on the dashboard which harkened back to another era.

The engine purred sweetly as he headed out of Brighton on the Lewes road. Hedgerows swept by, and every now and then a field of bright yellow flowers broke up the patches of vibrant green. He passed the old mill and a small stone church encrusted with moss. Beside the church was a cluster of ageing tombstones, some leaning at irregular angles, bent over with the passage of time. He liked driving in the country and promised himself he would put aside more time in the future to explore the Downs more thoroughly. Coming out here was like stepping back in time.

Soon after the turn-off to the charming little village of Bodwell, James found the narrow lane that led up in the direction of Castle Wilmington. Five miles on, a small wooden sign pointed the way to Firle Grove itself. It was a very secluded part of the Sussex countryside with leafy oaks and chestnuts forming a high canopy over the narrow roadway. Three cows looked up in unison as James drove his Morgan past the open metal gates marking the largely unheralded entrance to Castle Wilmington. The building itself was not visible from the road. A weathered brass plate with the name 'Elkington' embossed in black was the only evidence that James had come to the right place.

As he drove up the gravel drive he could see Sir Conrad waiting for him outside the main entrance, leaning on his trusty walking stick. As castles went, it was smaller than most, like Flavia had said, but it was still imposing in its own way. Stark and sharply rectangular, its roofline was defined by a long balustrade with a domed turret visible at one end. Lower down on adjoining levels there were other sections of balustrade as well. Two rows of elegant perpendicular windows graced the front of the building. A cluster of dark-leaved yews and oaks edged up against one side of the castle and its mottled stone walls were partially covered by some sort of ivy-like creeper. Small formal gardens filled with jonquils, daffodils and bluebells lined both sides of the stone path leading up to the front steps. Beneath a carved heraldic crest, a large oak door opened out into the main hallway.

Sir Conrad greeted him as he got out of the car.

'You made it, all right...' he said with a crusty grin. 'Flavia obviously gave you good instructions....'

He was wearing his old tweed jacket and an open-necked

shirt, and looked very much as he had the other night – every bit the eccentric aristocrat. He beckoned James to follow him as he made his way up the weathered stone steps.

Inside the hallway the tall, dimly-lit walls were decorated with large faded medieval tapestries mounted on heavy brass rods. Halfway down the hallway, on the left, was a tarnished coat of armour mounted on a stand, complete with a war-scarred helmet and vizor.

'This is Archie,' said Sir Conrad, pausing for a moment beside the coat of armour, which was considerably smaller than him. 'Archie was mortally wounded in the Battle of Bannockburn, poor fellow. An arrow got in through a gap in the chain mail. He was a distant relative, and this is all that's left of him, I'm sorry to say... apart from his bones in the ground. As you can see, fighting men were much smaller in those days...'

Sir Conrad moved on ahead, shuffling slightly to one side as he leaned on his carved walking stick. He led the way into a small room off the main hallway where there was a round wooden table and a selection of ageing armchairs. Above the open fireplace another ancestor, painted in oils and mounted in a crumbling gilt frame, gazed down on them. A cluster of fresh yellow daffodils had been placed in a small blue and white vase in front of the single open window that looked out onto the garden.

'Let's sit down in here for a moment,' said Sir Conrad. 'I'll show you around the castle later. There's quite a lot to see...'

James was reaching into his pocket for his tape-recorder when Sir Conrad's wife appeared in the doorway.

'Meet my wife, Olivia...' said Sir Conrad, turning round in his chair.

Lady Olivia came in to welcome him and James introduced himself. Like Sir Conrad she seemed to belong to another world, another time. Slim and tall like her husband, her grey-flecked hair had been pulled back into a long ponytail which extended halfway down her back. Lady Olivia had a pleasantly wrinkled face and twinkling blue eyes that were full of character. She was wearing a well-worn burgundy cardigan with occasional holes, and a long woollen skirt.

'I've been out in the garden,' she said cheerily. 'Clipping back a few of the climbing roses. They're getting out of hand. Would you like some tea or coffee..?'

James thanked her, requested coffee and pulled out his tape-recorder, placing it on the table. Lady Olivia left the two men to get started, closing the door behind her.

'You seemed very angry the other night,' said James, getting the interview under way. 'Angry that the Church was trying to wallpaper over some of the darkest episodes of the past...'

'Well, that's true in part,' said Sir Conrad reflectively. 'Obviously the Church is coming out in the open to some extent by admitting to the persecutions of the Inquisition....by putting all those implements of torture on show...'

He paused for a moment, glanced up at the ceiling as if gathering his thoughts, and then looked across at James.

'But there's more to it than that, if you look beneath the surface. I think there are many more secrets locked away inside the Vatican. Only the most obvious information – things that, for the most part, we already know – they're the only things coming out at this time...'

Lady Olivia came in with two mugs of coffee, a small jug of milk and a plate of irregular home-made biscuits, placed them on the table, and then departed.

'The crucial point,' said Sir Conrad, gesturing with his walking stick, 'is that at this special moment in history – the times we're living in, right now – all the spiritual undercurrents in the world seem to be surging towards some sort of climax. A powerful climax! Call it a clash of beliefs, call it what you will...As I see it, the most important spiritual battle is between the Church and the visionaries, between the Church and the heretics...'

'Tell me more,' said James, who wasn't quite sure where this was all heading.

Sir Conrad stared down at the table. His mood was suddenly tense. A few moments passed before he responded.

'Throughout recorded history, and in the Middle Ages in particular, the people who were branded as heretics... the people who were persecuted and put to death... very often these were the people who had a deeper vision of life. These were the people who understood the mystical realities of the world around them. But powerful organisations like the medieval Church were suspicious of these visionaries because they claimed to communicate directly with God. They were branded as heretics because they challenged the very authority of the Church...'

'And who exactly were these heretics and visionaries?' asked James.

'Well, in the Middle Ages,' said Sir Conrad, 'they included the Cathars and the Albigenses... heretics and dissenters in southern France. They also included all those poor witches, who were mostly simple folk living in the villages... country dwellers continuing the old pagan traditions of magic and healing. But it was the Cathars who were seen initially as the main threat. The Cathars were Christian Gnostics, Christian *perfecti*....Christian mystics who had a visionary approach to their religious practices. Gnostics are people who understand *gnosis* – spiritual knowledge, visionary spiritual experience... The Church actually mounted a Crusade against the Cathars in an effort to stamp them out completely. But although the Cathars were eventually rooted out and destroyed, the Church didn't really win....'

Sir Conrad paused to take a sip of coffee from his mug. James remembered Flavia's comment that her uncle viewed all of this as some sort of spiritual quest...

'The fight between the Church and the Gnostics has been going on for centuries...and it's still going on. It's still continuing, even now...'

'So, do you consider yourself a heretic?' asked James, searching for a quote that could perhaps underscore his article in the *Herald*.

'I am indeed a heretic, in the true sense of the word,' Sir Conrad said finally.

'I regard myself as a Gnostic...as a follower and practitioner of gnosis. That's what the Alpha and Omega is all about...'

Sir Conrad paused and asked James to turn off the tape recorder.

'The next part of our interview is not for publication in your paper. I hope I can trust you on that point...?'

James nodded in agreement, and Sir Conrad continued.

'We conduct various types of mystical and magical research here in the castle. We hold rituals which help open a path to what we regard as sacred realms of awareness... heightened levels of spiritual perception...call it what you will. We follow a universal path, a path which honours the gods and goddesses of all religions and mythologies. Later I'll take you upstairs to a special room we call the Sacred Space so you can see for yourself...'

A soft beam of mid-afternoon sunlight had settled suddenly on the forehead of the gilt-framed ancestor above the fireplace. Time was moving on. James finished his coffee.

'I should probably get back to the office soon to write my story...but it would be great to see the special room upstairs before I go...'

The old man nodded and James followed Sir Conrad as he rose to his feet, placed a firm hand on his carved walking stick, and headed towards the door. They walked together down the hallway until they reached an imposing wooden staircase, graced by an exquisitely carved banister.

'As we climb these stairs,' said Sir Conrad, 'you will notice several paintings, ornaments and sculptures that depict the gods and goddesses from different mythologies...' He smiled ironically. 'We give humble thanks to our Creator as we ascend these mystical heights...'

They went up to the first landing. A series of small, ornate shrines had been mounted on the castle walls, each decorated with drapes of exotic silk fabric which linked one shrine to the next. Each shrine contained small sculptures or paintings from the classical world mythologies.

'Here's a small bronze of the Greek god Apollo,' said Sir Conrad, pointing with the engraved handle of his walking stick as he paused in front of the first shrine. 'Apollo...god of purity and truth. Apollo is a sun god. He fills us with positive aspirations and brings us the power of healing when we need it...'

Then he cast his gaze further up the stairs, pointing to several other deities in turn.

'There's Zeus, the great decision maker, lord of the manifest universe... Mars, the great warrior god.... and Diana, goddess of the Moon...'

James thought the image of Diana was especially beautiful. The small, meticulous painting depicting her as a sacred hunter-goddess was edged in lustrous silver fabric and mounted in a silver metal frame, symbolic of the Moon.

Sir Conrad then pointed up to a high ledge overlooking the stairs. An impressive ancient Egyptian bust beamed down at them.

'That's Isis, the great enchantress. Goddess of the Mysteries...'

A little further up they reached a shrine containing a small marble sculpture of an unusual bird-headed god whose legs consisted of coiled snakes.

'That's a Graeco-Roman rendition of Abraxas,' said Sir Conrad. '... the Gnostic God of Time. Master of the 365 heavens...He was also known as Aeon or Zurvan....'

A few steps further took them past an exotic Aztec mask, a large unfurled scroll depicting Thoth and Osiris in the Egyptian Hall of Judgement and a small bronze sculpture of Hecate, goddess of the Greek underworld, who was shown with serpents writhing in her hair. They then passed a much larger sculpture of a primitive looking deity called Cernunnos, hewn from coarse, roughly textured stone. Horns protruded from his head.

Watching for James' response, Sir Conrad seemed to anticipate what he was thinking.

'That's not the Christian Devil,' he said quickly. 'Cernunnos is a Nature deity, the Celtic god of fertility and untamed creativity. As you can see, he has the head of a bull and the tail of a fish... he's the Lord and Master of all wild animals...'

On the highest landing they came finally to a tall wooden door, which was clearly different from all the other doors elsewhere in the castle. Fashioned from richly grained oak, it was inlaid with a variety of exotic magical motifs that had been skilfully carved from dark unpolished metal. A vivid mandala of brightly coloured feathers was mounted in the centre.

'And here is the room we refer to as the Sacred Space...' said Sir Conrad as he flicked a light switch and reached for the large ivory door handle.

'You are now about to enter one of our domed turrets... the turret you see as you first approach the castle ...'

The door opened into a blaze of vivid colours. The room itself was exactly square, but had a circular, domed ceiling. Each of the walls was draped in exotic, richly-textured fabrics which extended from the ceiling to the floor. The ceiling itself had been painted deep-blue, with a single golden circle running around the rim of the dome. In the apex of the dome was a six-pointed golden star whose beams extended down into a field of smaller silver stars which in turn spread out in all directions. The stars themselves were contained within the single golden circle.

'East is the direction of the rising sun,' said Sir Conrad, pointing to the wall directly opposite. 'East is the realm of new light by day, the source of our inspiration... Naturally, we have embellished this wall with beautiful yellow and golden fabrics.

They represent the mystical element Air.'

He turned to his right.

'South is the symbolic realm of Fire, the sphere of life-force and vitality. Its colours are all the different shades of red...'

He moved around to the next wall.

'Here we are facing West, which represents the element Water. This is the realm of dreams and deep emotions, which is linked symbolically to the Moon. As you can see, the fabrics covering this wall are all exquisite combinations of blue and silver...'

He turned once again.

'And now we are facing North, the sacred realm of Earth. Here we have chosen a wide range of earthen colours – greens, olives, browns, sepias, russet and black – to represent all the vital forces of Nature.

Sir Conrad pointed down to the smooth wooden floor, which had been painted deep blue, its design and colour an exact mirror-image of the ceiling. In the centre was a large golden star with smaller silver stars radiating out in all directions, contained, once again, within a golden circle.

'You may have heard of the sacred mystical axiom "As above, so below"... What this really means is that every human being – you, me, every sentient being – can learn, in time, to mirror the sacred universe. We all have that spark of sacred light, that spark of divinity, deep within us...'

He pointed to his heart.

'Our inner world is our pathway to the sacred. Here, in this special space, we honour the sacred gods and goddesses of all the mystic pantheons...'

James was impressed. He glanced around the room, taking it all in. For the moment he was totally lost for words. He had never seen anything quite like the interior of this castle and it was quite something to be shown something like this. For all his eccentricities, he really liked Sir Conrad and he respected his integrity. He would never betray the secrets he had been shown. Fortunately there was more than enough in what Sir Conrad had told him earlier about medieval heretics to help him flesh out his article for the *Herald*.

As they walked slowly downstairs, glancing again at each of the shrines in turn, James thought to himself how extraordinary it was to be able to create such an inspiring and magical environment within one's own home. Admittedly, Sir Conrad and his wife had a whole castle at their disposal, but the upper reaches of the building, with its shrines and symbolic embellishments, were very special indeed.

'Would you like to come to one of our mystical gatherings? ' asked Sir Conrad when they reached the foot of the stairs.

'I would indeed...' said James. 'I'd like that very much...'

'Excellent...I thought you might be interested...I'll confirm everything with Flavia and one of us will get in touch soon...'

James was about to leave when he remembered that he had some information about church politics that Sir Conrad might find fascinating.

'By the way,' he said, pausing in the doorway. 'I made a tape-recording of a conversation I overheard at the exhibition...a conversation between Giuseppe Martino and Father Rotheram....It's about an ancient biblical text that the Vatican wants to keep secret. I'll make a copy for you and bring it with me when I come...'

'That sounds interesting,' said Sir Conrad with a wry grin on his face. '... very interesting indeed...'

James waved farewell and set off down the path. He liked it here and it would be good to come back soon. As he climbed into his car he felt suddenly different, as if part of him had changed. Something inside him had definitely stirred, although just at this moment he couldn't be sure exactly what it was.

16

BACK AT THE OFFICE, finalising the article on heretics and the Inquisition proved to be no problem at all. He already had all the basic details and the profile of Giuseppe Martino backed up on his hard drive. The interview with Sir Conrad was all that had to be added. Soon he had over two thousand words. Finished, complete...straight in to Jo for her perusal. He glanced at his watch. 6.25, Friday afternoon. A good day's work...

But Libby had wanted to talk just as he was finishing it.

'Sorry, not now...'

'When, then?'

'Soon... I don't know...'

'What's wrong, James? It's like you're trying to avoid me...'

In a way, he was. He had other things on his mind right now.

He rummaged in an atlas which he found in the *Herald* reference library. The voice on the taped conversation had made a reference to a church mission at some place called Shocmil. And there was mention of a lake. Atlan or Etlan is what it had sounded like, the voices were a bit muffled. He found a map of Guatemala. Guatemala City was obvious enough, right there in the heart of the country. He scanned his eyes across the map from one side to the other. There was a large lake in the western highlands, Lago de Atitlán. That must be it. The only other notable lake was Lago de Izabel on the other side of the country. But there was no sign of any town called Shocmil, or anything remotely like it.

He looked for the towns around Lago de Atitlán. He located Santiago Atitlán on the southern shores of the lake. Cerro de Ora and San Lucas Tolimán were further around. Santa Catarina Palopó and San Antonio Palopó in the east, Panajachel across the lake to the north. San Pedro La Laguna and San Pablo La Laguna over on the western shore. Great sounding places but no sign or hint of Shocmil...

He decided to go out for a coffee.

Libby followed him...

'James, wait...'

'Not now...'

'Please, James...'

'Well, all right then...'

They sat down at the same table at Ziggi's, facing each other. The table by the window.

He stayed quiet, caught up in his thoughts.

She came over and sat next to him. Then she huddled up against him, nudging him gently.

'What's the matter, James?' she asked him, 'Suddenly it's like you've become a total stranger...'

'Sorry,' he said. 'It's nothing personal. I've just been thinking about other things...'

'About Flavia Timmins ?' she asked him.

'No,' he said. 'No...

'Well, yes.

'She's part of it...' he added a moment later.

'But it's not just her...'

He decided to tell Libby about his visit to Wilmington Castle. Just the basic details. The fascinating interview with Lord Elkington. Well, he thought it was fascinating anyway. At the same time he took special care to make no mention whatever of Sir Conrad's mystical inclinations, the Sacred Space, or the shrines in the castle. Those details would remain a secret...

'I was searching for Shocmly,' he said randomly, as the waitress brought two cappucinos to the table.

* * *

After he finished his coffee he left Libby at Ziggi's and went home by himself. He knew he was making her unhappy but he just couldn't help it.

Soon after he got home the phone rang. It was Flavia.

'Found your name in the phone book,' she said cheerily. 'You're the only James Highgate in the whole of Brighton....'

'Guess that's true,' said James. It was great to hear her voice. He could picture her now. The wonderful auburn hair. The coffee-olive skin. That exotic look. The wonderful smile.

'How have you been?' he said, not sure quite how to begin.

'It's more like how have *you* been?' she said breezily. 'Uncle Conrad told me you paid him a visit at the castle...

'I did. It was fascinating. Totally fascinating...'

'Want to get together to tell me more ?' she asked. Simple. Direct. He liked that.

'Sure. When?'

'How about later tonight? Say, around nine in the White Hog bar. Where we were with Marley...'

That was fine, let's do that.

James put the phone down. He was suddenly very pleased with himself. This could be heading somewhere, he thought to himself, although he wasn't quite sure where. But meeting Flavia alone in the White Hog bar was definitely a good start...

It was still over two hours before they would be getting together...

He made himself a light snack, sat down and started drumming his fingers on the coffee table. He thought again about the castle and all the extraordinary things that must go on there. Then he remembered the tape. Reaching into his jacket pocket he retrieved it and put it into his machine to make a copy. Sir Conrad would be really interested to hear this...

When that was done there was still time to kill, so he decided to go for a stroll around the Lanes. It was always a great place to explore in the early evening. Wonderful aromas of garlic and spices from the numerous little restaurants, sounds of distant laughter and wafting night music... with a little imagination it was almost like being in Italy or southern France. He shuffled around the narrow streets, looking into the boutique windows.

He arrived at the White Hog half an hour early and got himself a drink.

Everyone around him at the bar was having a great time. Bluesy jazz was piping its way through the bar, ahead of tonight's live band. He waited impatiently for Flavia to arrive.

When she breezed in she was totally gorgeous, with still that hint of mystery that he found so attractive. She was wearing a fluffy high-neck pullover and light blue jeans. Dead simple, nothing especially exotic. But Flavia would look like a goddess whatever she was wearing...

He got her a chardonnay with ice, just like the other night.

Mustn't look too interested, he told himself. Stay a bit cool. Flavia likes to keep a bit of distance. Take it one step at a time...

'Tell me everything,' she said. Simple and direct again. Where to begin?

'I got on really well with Sir Conrad,' said James. '... and the castle is totally amazing. I'm fascinated to know more about the mystical rituals that go on in the Sacred Space...'

'Did Uncle Conrad take you up there?'

'He did. And he also invited me to come over one night so I can take part...get a taste of it. That's something maybe I can work out with you...'

He sipped on his drink and looked casually around the bar. The subtle and enticing sounds of Norah Jones were wafting above the murmurings of the crowd ... 'Come away with me...'

'Great, isn't it...' said Flavia, catching his thoughts. 'Another one of those wonderful blues women...'

She looked at him quizzically, pulling back just a little. That fascinating ability to retreat into herself, thought James to himself.

'Did you get a sense of something sacred, something truly mystical up there at the castle?' she asked suddenly, becoming more serious. She was watching him. Intently. He could feel those hazel brown eyes probing him. Watching. Sensing his mood...

'I did...but first tell me a bit more about you...'

He wanted to change the subject, find out more about her.

'I'm a linguist... I'm good with languages....I'm fluent in Spanish, Italian, German.... Although my background is mostly English and I was born here – I actually grew up here in Brighton – my grandmother was Spanish, my mother half-Italian. I guess it's in my blood...'

'So being a linguist is your actual work? Is that what you do?'

'I do some translation work on a regular basis. I teach overseas students who come over here to Brighton from the Continent and need help with their courses. I also help out in the law courts when they need a translator...'

She paused and smiled.

'But my real work is up at the castle. That's what I care most about...'

'So why is that so important to you?' asked James, probing just a little. She really was a totally fascinating and very unusual person, quite apart from her exotic physical beauty. He wondered if she realized just how attractive she was.

'I'm sure we'll get to that later...' she said, looking aside and then catching his eye as she turned back again.

She leaned back on her chair, listening to the music in the bar, allowing herself to become absorbed in the enticing rhythms for just a brief moment.

'Do you like this sort of music?' she asked him. 'Do you get into the rhythm...?'

James nodded.

'I love blues and jazz. And reggae. All that sort of music. That's why Marley and I get along so well...'

'Have you ever ridden on the drum beat ... ridden away into another realm, another place? '

James didn't know quite how to respond. He'd never thought of drum rhythms in quite that way.

Flavia didn't wait for his response.

'That's what we're doing next week up at the castle,' she said teasingly, expecting him to be surprised.

'We're learning how to ride on the drum beat and call the spirits. We're learning how to ride into the mystical world. All on the beat of a drum...'

James took another sip from his glass. It was nearly empty but he didn't want to go to the bar and get another drink just now. He just wanted to sit at the table and look across at her. Watch her. Listen to everything she was saying. It was all totally amazing. He had never met anyone remotely like her before.

'... On the beat of a drum...?' he asked.

'Everyone... you, me...we can all learn to ride a drum beat into the mystical world,' she said simply and mysteriously, as if it was the most obvious thing in the world. 'That's when our dreams come alive...'

Later, after they left the White Hog, James walked her to her car. He thought about kissing her lightly on the cheek, but decided against it.

She got in and wound down the window.

'See you on Tuesday night, up the castle.' she said sweetly. 'Around eight...'

17

A SOFT AMBER GLOW washed across the fields and hedgerows as James drove his Morgan up the gravel drive at Wilmington Castle. He was twenty minutes early. Lady Olivia welcomed him at the door and invited him in. There was no sign of any other visitors. No sign either of Sir Conrad or Flavia. Lady Olivia ushered him down the hallway to the room with the ageing armchairs and asked him to wait. She'd come and collect him when they were ready.

He sat and watched as the shadows cast by the setting sun lengthened across the ancestor in the crumbling gilt frame. James was becoming a little restless. Nervous, perhaps, in anticipation... Wondering what to expect...

As the last vestiges of filtered sunlight disappeared from the room, Lady Olivia came to get him. She had changed out of her more familiar clothes and was wearing a long flowing white gown, drawn in around the waist with a thick band of golden braid. With her flecked grey hair pulled back in a long pony tail she looked almost medieval. James imagined her as a figure from the court of King Arthur, or some other bygone era. She held her forefinger to her lips to request silence and motioned for him to follow her.

Together they ascended the mystical staircase. Once again James looked on in fascination as they passed the shrines of all the gods and goddesses: Apollo, Zeus, Mars, Diana, Isis, Abraxas, Thoth, Osiris, Hecate, Cernunnos... he was fascinated by them all.

Finally they came to the top landing and paused outside the regal oak door with the inlaid magical motifs and the feather mandala. Gateway to the Sacred Space...

Lady Olivia drew him aside.

'When you enter the Sacred Space,' she whispered to him

softly, 'lie down in the centre of the room and just relax. Breathe deeply. Absorb what happens. Focus on your awareness. Stay open. Allow yourself to flow with everything you experience...'

She knocked quietly on the door and then eased it open herself.

She led him in.

Across the room, in the Eastern quarter, a large single candle had been given pride of place, providing the only available light. Intriguing shadows danced across the fabric-lined walls of the room. James glanced quickly around. There were perhaps eight or nine people here, none of whom he knew. Like Lady Olivia they were wearing long white gowns.

He lay down on the floor in the centre of the room, and looked up towards the dome, fixing his attention on the large golden hexagram and the field of smaller silver stars...

Meanwhile the people in the room had begun clustering around him. Then they sat down, cross-legged, forming themselves into an oval configuration rather like the shape of a canoe. Soon they had enclosed him completely, allowing a small amount of space on either side.

A gowned female figure now came in from the landing. She closed the door behind her and knelt beside him in silence. It was Flavia. She lay down beside him on the floor without saying a word.

Silence, once again

But it wasn't long before the door was once again thrust open, as Sir Conrad entered in regal style. James could see him quite clearly, marked out in stark profile against the soft light filtering in from the landing. Similarly clad in a long white gown, he was wearing a spectacular headband of vividly-coloured feathers and was beating on a large flat drum.

After making his grand entrance Sir Conrad placed the drum carefully on the ground and grasped what appeared to be a large gourd rattle. Moving silently to the far side of the room he then raised the rattle high in the air and swept it down from head to toe, shaking it vigorously from side to side. This was clearly a call for the spirits to attend. Above the raucous din of the spirit-rattle Sir Conrad's booming voice sounded rich and sonorous:

I call the spirits of East,
Spirits of the rising sun...
We seek your guiding presence, here in our Sacred Space...
We welcome you here tonight. We welcome you in peace...

Shaking his rattle in rhythmic fashion he now moved around to the South, building with each footstep a protective circle of sound...

I call the spirits of South,
Spirits of Fire...

He then moved around to the West, extending the encircling arc of sound still further with every beat of his gourd rattle...

I call the spirits of West,
Spirits of our deepest dreams and our most profound emotions...

And then finally to the last quarter...

I call the spirits of North,
Spirits of the living Earth...

Then it was all done, the circle of sacred sound complete...

Sir Conrad passed the rattle to Flavia and picked up the large flat drum. All the while James could sense the welcoming presence of the people who had come here tonight. Surrounding him, protecting him, enclosing him.... He noticed that they were all facing towards the East, facing in the direction of the rising sun....a spirit-canoe with its spirit-voyagers, bound together like a union of souls, brought together for a sacred purpose.

Sir Conrad started beating on his drum. Deep, sensual drumming — repetitive drumming that sounded like the heartbeat of an ancient spirit-ancestor. Drumming that echoed from the very depths of space, drumming from the heart of an archaic, living dream. James felt he was being transported, carried along.... borne like a leaf, floating in a stream. And still the drumming continued....

And now Flavia began shaking her rattle as well, pulsing with the mysterious drum-beat as if she were accompanying her uncle on some sort of spirit-journey. This continued for some time and then seemed to reach a climax. She raised herself up and then knelt down, resting her rattle upon the floor. Then she crossed her arms as if clutching a living creature to her breast, drawing it up into her cupped hands. Reaching down, she placed her cupped hands on James' forehead and blew hard through her fingers against his skin.

Then she whispered in his ear.

'I have given you a spirit-helper. A spirit that brings truth and understanding....A spirit-helper to guide you on your journey of the soul...'

She paused briefly and then whispered to him once again.

'Imagine this spirit-helper in your mind's eye,' she urged him softly. 'Open your inner being to its living presence, and then you will see it...'

Flavia reached down so she was very close to him now. He could sense the intimate warmth of her skin, smell the soft fragrance of her hair. She cupped her hands above his chest and once again blew hard through her fingers as if transmitting some sort of magical power into every pore of his body.

Again she whispered to him. 'Open your inner being to its living presence, and then you will see it...

And, indeed, he could see it now... fluttering joyously above his head. A small exotic bird with a vivid red breast, long green tail feathers and a vibrant golden crest! In some mysterious and inexplicable way it seemed to be calling him. Calling him through its magical and enchanting song! Dancing in the air before his eyes, cascading its vibrant feathers in an arc of radiant light... his very own Bird of Paradise..!

James felt a deep sense of peace surge up within him, a feeling quite different from anything he had ever experienced before. And now the very boundaries of his body seemed to be dissolving... dissolving into a welcoming haze of soft diffuse light. He knew then that he had come to a different place, that he had entered a quite different level of awareness. That he had ventured, unmistakeably, into some sort of sacred territory...

Gradually he awoke and opened his eyes. Flavia was looking down at him, smiling.

He felt suddenly very close to her, as if they had shared something intimate and special.

'How was that?' she asked, beaming down at him.

'It was wonderful...really wonderful. I saw the spirit-helper you found for me...it called out to me...'

Sir Conrad, meanwhile, had begun beating his drum rapidly in all four directions, thanking the spirits for their attendance before releasing them to their mystic realms. He seemed very much in his element here... the sage and heretic with his loyal band of followers...

Later they gathered downstairs for light refreshments. Sir Conrad was keen to learn what James had experienced during the spirit-drumming. He drew him aside, anxious to hear what he had to say. Flavia was listening attentively as well. James then recounted how he had seen a small exotic bird with a vivid red breast, his very own Bird of Paradise with long green tail feathers and a vibrant golden crest... It had seemed to be calling out to him. Singing in a special, very personal sort of way...

Sir Conrad smiled knowingly, as if all of this was very

familiar territory.

'The spirit-helpers are our magical allies,' he said reassuringly. 'When you open the sacred path the spirit-helpers will always be there to guide you...'

He looked fixedly at James, a twinkle in his bright blue eyes.

'We must find out where your spirit-bird came from, and why it chose you in particular!'

Then he turned away to talk with some of the others. He wanted to know what they had experienced with the spirit-canoe... how they had felt as the drumming propelled them into a different world...

'Riding the drum-beat is a special skill,' he reminded them, '...and obviously it takes a bit of practice. But riding the drum-beat can be very special. Riding the drum-beat opens the way to the spirit world...'

Most of them had now started making their way out of the castle. Flavia, Olivia and Sir Conrad were talking among themselves in the hallway.

James remembered he had brought the tape from Caxton Hall.

'Here's the tape I told you about,' he said, retrieving it from his jacket pocket. 'The most fascinating part is the reference to the ancient Christian text....the text the Vatican wants to keep secret at all costs...'

He passed it over to Sir Conrad.

'The actual text is being scrutinised somewhere in Guatemala... in a church mission somewhere near a place called Lake Atitlán...'

James then thanked his hosts and got ready to leave. Flavia walked with him to the door.

'That was very special,' she said to him, drawing him just a little closer and locking her arm inside his. She looked at him intently. Her enticing and mysterious look.

'We'll get together again soon...'

18

BACK AT THE *HERALD* there was no doubt about it. Jo was really buzzing. He hadn't seen her like this for quite a while. Response to the feature story on the Inquisition had been excellent. Jo thought it was great...really great. Something really different, something right out of the ordinary. Circulation was up. Advertising was up. She was really pleased with the way the paper was turning around.

But right now James was finding it hard to concentrate. Especially on all the little news items that had to be shaped into feature articles. It was hard staying focused after what he had experienced at the castle. It was hard keeping his mind attuned to the everyday flow after tapping into something truly magical....however brief that glimpse had been.

He chewed on the end of his pen and then shuffled his collection of notes-in-progress once more around his desk. They were arranged in individual heaps. There was an article to write on Singaporean doctors separating Siamese twins who were joined at the head, a virtually impossible operation. A piece based on Bill Clinton's autobiography relating his version of the affair with Monica Lewinsky. The latest antics of Elton John. Rod Stewart crooning his way through the old standards. The new Russian tennis stars at Wimbledon...

The dead eye of his blank computer screen stared back at him.

He thought about Flavia as he looked across the office at Libby. There she was, hard at work on her laptop. She had virtually ignored him the last couple of days, which was fair enough after the way he had treated her. She said she was working on a piece on genetically modified crops. It was getting to be a real slog...she'd hardly had time to think about anything else. Well, maybe... Even bubbly receptionist Rachael was looking subdued after being jilted on a date.

Then James remembered he hadn't seen Marley for several days. Poor old Marley. Still pining for Jo, and here she was firing up on all cylinders without him...

The phone rang. He thought it might be Flavia – two whole days had passed since he'd seen her – but instead it was Sir Conrad Elkington. He'd listened to the tape. *Fascinating, just fascinating...* He'd like to talk. Could he come by the office tomorrow afternoon....maybe spend a few minutes and have a chat in the park...? Somewhere a bit private, out of the way... The park would be quiet at that time of day...

Next day at the agreed time, James slipped out of the office. Sir Conrad was waiting for him, leaning on his ever-dependable walking stick. He was wearing the same tweed jacket as always but had added a deerstalker cap to his repertoire. They strolled together along the seafront and then down Grand Parade, passing the exotic Royal Pavilion, which looked more like a fairytale Indian palace than an icon of local Brighton architecture. Whoever had designed its elaborate spires and decorative embellishments had a distinctly whimsical sense of humour and a truly magical imagination! The park lay just beyond the ornate building, a little further on.

They found a bench in a secluded area of the park beside a weeping willow and a cluster of white and purple irises. As Sir Conrad had anticipated, there was no-one around. He wanted to talk to James about the tape recording.

'You found the tape interesting?' said James. 'I thought you would...'

'Giuseppe Martino is right,' he replied, getting straight to the point, '...that discovery in Guatemala really is political dynamite. Anything biblical actually written in Aramaic is *early*....really early.'

He paused and rested his walking stick against the bench. He wanted James to know how truly significant this all was.

'Aramaic was the language spoken by Jesus. It's central to the whole thing. Everything we know about the Bible and divine revelation would have to be revised... and that shakes at the very foundations! The earliest versions of the four main gospels were written in Greek which shows they come later on the time-scale...'

He gazed out across the park and smiled as he noticed a couple of pigeons competing for territory on the grass....power struggles taking place on all levels of existence...

'I wonder exactly why they're so rattled about this alternative version of the Second Coming?' he said. 'It must be truly radical if Cardinal Ratzinger wants to keep it hidden under wraps....'

James nodded in agreement. It was indeed a fascinating issue, and quite possibly revolutionary. But he had to concede privately that at this particular moment he was much more interested in asking Sir Conrad about what he had experienced at the castle the other night. He wanted to find out more about the spirit-helpers and the whole idea of sacred space. How Sir Conrad had built that protective circle of magical sound....

'What did you mean when you spoke about opening the sacred path?' asked James, moving their conversation away from the Vatican just for a moment.

'Exactly that...' said Sir Conrad. 'When you ride on the shaman's drum-beat you enter the spirit world. You enter sacred space. The drum-beat literally transports you...'

He looked searchingly at James and seemed pensive for just a moment.

'Do you understand why the gods and goddesses are so important?' he asked suddenly, changing tack for a moment.

James shook his head. He had no idea, specifically. He assumed that myths and legends were just fascinating and creative stories... that the ancient idea of gods and goddesses belonged to another era, a time of legend and fable long lost in the past.

'The gods are goddesses are alive!' said Sir Conrad emphatically, clenching his fist for effect. He turned quickly around to see if anyone else was listening, but fortunately the park remained deserted.

'The gods and goddesses are alive within us,' he said, emphasizing his point once more. 'They represent our sacred potential....everything we can hope to become...'

James was listening attentively. He greatly respected Sir Conrad and his mystical ideas, but it still sounded rather theoretical. He looked puzzled, unsure how to respond.

Sir Conrad could tell he was unconvinced.

'Would you like me to demonstrate what I mean?'

James nodded.

Sir Conrad sat poised upon the park bench, closed his eyes, and took several deep breaths.

In an instant he had withdrawn deep within himself, as if entering a deep meditation. Then he was suddenly extremely still... frozen in the silence of the moment.

Now as James looked on in amazement, enthralled by all that he could see in the clear light of day, Sir Conrad seemed to change his very form and structure from deep within. It was almost like casting off the constraints of one's outer appearance in order to take on another. Changing bodies, like changing clothes....changing from a human being into the archetypal form of an ancient god...

In a remarkable transition the very shape and essence of Sir Conrad's body seemed to undergo a total transformation. Where once had sat an eccentric English aristocrat there now sat a fully robed Egyptian deity, the ibis-headed god who presided over the Hall of Judgement... *the Great God Thoth!*

James was utterly amazed. He could hardly believe what he was seeing. The familiar and much-admired Sir Conrad had completely disappeared from view. In a unique and tantalizing instant he had been utterly and totally replaced by an ancient Egyptian god. Alive and tangible and sitting motionless...on a park bench in Brighton!

It was completely beyond James' rational understanding. He had never experienced anything like this before.

But then the vision started to fade. The long black beak of the ibis-headed god was gradually replaced by the cheery, pink-faced profile of the elderly English gentleman and soon the Egyptian robes in turn also faded from view and were replaced by the familiar tweed jacket. Sir Conrad Elkington had returned.

'How did you do that?' asked James, struggling to make sense of it all. 'How on Earth did you do that...?'

'Effective, isn't it...' said Sir Conrad with an ironic grin on his face. 'It's actually quite easy when you know how. We call it "assuming the God-form". It's a central practice in magical visualisation. It all comes down to the power of the will... the power of the imagination...'

James was lost for words.

'As you imagine, so you become,' said Sir Conrad enigmatically. 'That's the very essence of magic...'

They walked slowly towards the seafront, and arrived back at the *Herald*. Then just as he was about to disappear upstairs and return to his desk Sir Conrad drew him aside. There was one more thing he wanted to tell him.

'That spirit-helper, that exotic bird you saw the other night...'

James nodded enthusiastically. Of course, he remembered it vividly.

'It was a quetzal bird,' he said. 'The quetzal bird is highly revered by the Mayans of Guatemala. It's considered sacred. In fact, it's their national icon. As I mentioned the other night, we will have to find out why it chose you in particular...'

* * *

Around mid-morning the next day James got another call at the office. It was Sir Conrad again, phoning from the castle.

'I've been thinking,' he said excitedly. 'There really is a fascinating pattern emerging in all this.... everything's starting to fall into place. Have you got a moment..?'

James said that was fine. He took a sip of coffee from his mug. It was already getting cold. He'd been drinking it for the last twenty minutes.

'Consider the situation...' said Sir Conrad. 'Consider the different parts of the jigsaw and how we've stumbled upon it...'

James was doing his best to pay attention. It was a pity about the coffee, but at least he was feeling more focused than this time yesterday...

'Think about this sequence of events and tell me what you think. The drumming begins and we call our spirit-helpers... a Mayan quetzal bird appears during your drum journey and communicates with you in a very special sort of way ... meanwhile, a revolutionary biblical text has turned up in Guatemala – an ancient text that the Vatican wants to keep secret – and the text itself contains tantalising possibilities about the Second Coming....'

He paused for a moment to see if James was keeping up with him. For the moment, he wasn't.

'It all points to an early follower of Jesus – or maybe even Jesus himself – visiting Central America at the very beginning of the Christian era...'

James was beginning to catch the drift of it all. Here was Sir Conrad shifting the boundaries yet again, venturing into totally uncharted territory... But Sir Conrad obviously believed he was really onto something. Something really significant...

'There's something else...,' he said. 'Something which possibly provides the key to the whole question...'

James remained silent, allowing him to continue.

'Have you heard about the famous Mayan calendar? Did you know that the Mayans had the most advanced calendar in the ancient world...?'

James hadn't heard about that.

'No,' he said. 'Tell me about it...'

Sir Conrad continued. He was really excited now, James could tell from the tone of his voice...

'Well, the ancient Mayans charted the passage of time over a period of 5,128 years, and they did it in a way that was more exact than at any time before or since. According to the Mayan astronomers, the Calendar ends on the 21st of December, 2012...'

'.....ends?' asked James

'That date marks the end of time,' said Sir Conrad, driving home the point.

'...the end of the world as we know it. I think we may have found the date for the Second Coming...'

'That's extraordinary,' said James. '...that's really amazing...'

'I've had an idea...,' said Sir Conrad. 'I want to take this further. I really think we're on to something here. Perhaps the biggest story of our time...'

He paused to make sure that James was really listening.

'I think you should go to Guatemala to check it all out...'

James was amazed, dumbfounded. It was all moving too quickly.

'Have a think about it...,' he said. 'I'll speak to you tomorrow...'

19

WHEN JAMES ARRIVED at the *Herald* the next morning he was surprised to see that Sir Conrad had already got there before him. He was sitting in Jo's office, deeply engaged in serious conversation. And Flavia was there as well.

'Hope you don't mind, old chap,' said Sir Conrad as James walked in.

'Strike while the iron's hot and all that...'

Flavia gave him one of her exotic, teasing smiles as he sat down to join them.

Jo looked across at James. She had that very focused look that he had come to both love and fear. She was thinking stories. She was thinking feature stories. She was thinking *big* feature stories...

'Sir Conrad's been telling me all about this Guatemala idea. I must say, the possibility of turning up an ancient biblical text in the depths of the Central American jungle does sound pretty exotic...'

James nodded in vague approval, although he wasn't actually sure if it was discovered in the jungle. On the map he had looked at Lake Atitlán was in the western highlands and a caption said it was a sunken volcanic crater. Still, he wasn't going to argue about that minor detail, especially if there was a good story to be uncovered. He hadn't had his first cup of coffee yet so his brain was not yet in full throttle.

'Sir Conrad says he is willing to pay for you to go to Guatemala to check it all out,' said Jo. 'And we will get a world-rights exclusive to run the story in the *Herald*. He thinks you might need to be away for around four or five weeks...'

'That's all well and good...,' said James quickly gathering his thoughts so they made some kind of sense. '... but how will I get around? How will I actually communicate with anyone? I've never been to Guatemala before...'

He paused to consider.

'And I don't speak Spanish...'

'Flavia does,' said Jo. 'She's offered to go as well....she's offered to help out as your translator...'

Flavia smiled across at him, in her unique, conspiratorial manner. With both Sir Conrad and Flavia scheming against him, James knew he had no chance.

'OK, fine...' he said weakly, hoping his inspiration would return soon. He knew it was just his regular need for caffeine. He really needed it at ground-breaking moments like this. Maybe Guatemala would prove to be the chance of a lifetime but it still felt like the wrong time of the morning to talk about it. How could he make such important decisions before having his first coffee of the day?

'Sorted...,' said Jo, gathering her notes together on her desk and bringing the meeting to the close.

She smiled sweetly as Sir Conrad and Flavia got ready to leave.

'Thank you again for your great initiative, Sir Conrad. It's great to have some encouragement from a local reader of the *Herald*...'

James had to admit it. Jo definitely knew how to be charming and deferential when it came to PR.

As they walked through the office on their way to the door, Flavia put her arm around James and gave him a little hug.

'Won't it be great,' she gushed enthusiastically. 'Just imagine... tracking down shamans in Guatemala! Tracking down secret biblical texts locked away in a remote Catholic Mission deep in the heart of the jungle...'

James had to admit that it did all sound pretty extraordinary...

He smiled back at her but then, just at that very moment, he caught Libby's eye beaming in on him across the room.

He realised then that Libby had been watching every move as

they had come out of Jo's office. Now she would know for sure that there really was something special going on between the two conspirators, James Highgate and Flavia Timmins...

Feeling distinctly uncomfortable, he quickly looked away.

Libby bit on her lip, feeling totally rejected. Any warmth or tenderness she felt for James had been suddenly poisoned. Utterly and totally...

She would never speak to him again, or at least, she would keep any communications between them strictly to a minimum.

She looked down at her notes and then back up at her computer screen. Mining in the Alaskan wilderness...the Kyoto Protocol...Japanese whaling in the Antarctic....What did it all matter? Suddenly she didn't care about anything any more. Bloody men! Why did they always let you down like this....?

Meanwhile James was busy talking with Sir Conrad and Flavia over by the reception desk, saying his farewells as they were leaving the office. He closed the glass door quietly behind them as they departed.

On the way back to his desk he glanced furtively across at Libby and then looked quickly away again. Part of him still wanted to explain, but there was really nothing to say. It was all very unfortunate and he hadn't meant to hurt her feelings.

Looking away so she wouldn't make eye-contact, Libby reached down beside her desk and gathered her bag. Then she quietly slipped out of the office. She needed some time by herself to gather her thoughts and get her focus back on her stories.

It was time to go back to Ziggi's. It was time for a really strong black coffee. *Alone.* Later she might go down to the Black Crow and hang out with one of the exciting new writers they were promoting this weekend ... Something was bound to turn up...a new writer from SoHo?

ço∾ço

Part Three

Kukulcan

ço∾ço

20

THEY HAD ARRIVED in Guatemala City. Flavia had insisted on separate bedrooms. A professional trip, she had called it. They had to get their priorities right, at least for the time being...

James looked out of the hotel window into the street below. It wasn't exactly the best part of town, but then he had to admit that he was being paid to be here. When he had seen the name of the hotel, Casa Presidente, listed on the flight itinerary he had had flashes of something exotic, something really grand and regal. How easy it was to get taken in, just by the allure of a name! Across the road the skyline was dominated by grubby run-down apartments with washing hanging out to dry on the balcony. A posse of teenage youths was playing football in the street and an old American car had had its front wheels and doors removed, just three doors down. James seriously doubted whether he would find any shamans here...

Flavia had told him not to worry. The hotel might not have much going for it, but it was the best they could do at short notice. All the larger hotels were booked out for conferences. At least Uncle Conrad had arranged for them to get a driver to take them out to Panajachel. From that point on they would have to find their own way to Father Delgado's mission. Luis would be coming to get them in the morning after breakfast, she had said He would lend us a mobile phone so we could call him if we got into any difficulties. Don't fret, she had told him. Relax. Enjoy yourself. Remember, this is an adventure...

Luis arrived just as James was finishing his omelette. He was short and neatly dressed and was wearing an impeccably-pressed white cotton shirt, open at the neck. The name of his hire-car company, Astro, was emblazoned in blue and gold letters on his shirt, just below the left lapel. His dark hair was cut short with a mathematically precise parting just right of centre. Luis spoke good English, with just a hint of a West Coast American accent. He had been in this situation before. He could spot foreign tourists who were well and truly out of their depth.

'First visit to Guatemala ma'am,' he asked?'... 'Here, let me help you with that...' He reached down for her suitcase... 'Good morning, sir, sorry I'm a little early, go right ahead and finish your breakfast...'

At least he was punctual and knew what he was doing, even if the modest hotel breakfast had been cut short by his arrival. James felt suddenly confident that they would arrive in Panajachel in one piece.

Luis went on ahead and carried the suitcases out through the hotel lobby to the waiting four-wheel drive. Like its driver, it too was impeccable. Gleaming metallic blue, with chrome wheels and glistening hubcaps and not a hint of dust... For the moment it dominated the narrow inner city streetscape like a proud monument. It certainly stood out in marked contrast to the desecrated and abandoned American car just across the street. Luis leered across at a couple of loitering youths, daring them to lay a finger on his shiny wagon. They moved quickly away. Then he went ahead and loaded up the car. Two elderly women who had been putting out the washing watched him from one of the balconies across the way. It was rare for such gleaming luxury to put in an appearance at the Casa Presidente.

Soon they were heading out on the main highway behind a procession of trucks and overcrowded buses, the smell of diesel fumes billowing into the air. James caught a brief glimpse of the impressive Palacio Nacional in the city centre and there were some fine, palm-lined boulevards. But essentially this seemed to be a city like so many other modern sprawling cities, burdened down by petrol fumes that were poisoning its life-blood.

'Most people who come here don't choose that downtown district where you were staying,' said Luis breezily as they drove west on Centroamérica 1. 'Antigua is much nicer, with its colonial architecture and cobblestone streets. Visitors prefer to go there...'

He was sounding like a regular tour guide now, but James and Flavia didn't really mind. It was all part of the journey. Luis continued with his commentary.

'Antigua was the original capital but it was devastated in 1773. That's when the earthquakes came. You can still see many of the ruins...'

As Luis was talking James remembered something that tour guides were inclined to overlook, that Guatemala was a country ravaged not only by earthquakes but also by military revolts. He had read in the newspaper how the country had gone through a civil war lasting 36 years, and that over 200,000 lives had been lost. Despite its exotic appeal it seemed to be a country burdened by ongoing tragedy...

Flavia, though, was taking everything in her stride. For the moment she was content to simply look out of the window and let Luis do all the concentrating. It was certainly a major operation weaving in and out of the heavy, congested traffic.

At different times through the hurtling stream of trucks and buses they could see the three volcanoes that marked the distinctive horizon beyond the city outskirts – Volcán Acatenango ahead of them in the west, Volcán Fuego – the mountain of fire – off to the southwest and still showing its sultry red plumes and Volcán Agua away in the southeast. Soon they passed the turnoff to Antigua, a short distance west of Guatemala City, but decided not to stop. Best to head on to Panajachel, they both agreed. Best get there as soon as possible...

Soon they had reached Tecpán and were making their way towards the Los Encuentros junction. Then they turned off the main highway and drove down into Sololá on the way to Panajachel. In Sololá they stopped to catch a brief glimpse of the busy marketplace in the plaza beside the cathedral. It was the first time they had seen so many exotic Mayan women all in one place together. The women had come in from the surrounding villages to trade their flowers and vegetables, and were wearing their distinctive, richly- coloured *huipil* shawls.

'This is more like it,' said Flavia, breathing in the atmosphere. It was good to be finally well away from all the fumes and gridlock on the highway. Here in the marketplace there were quite different smells to absorb – richly scented flowers, tropical fruits, farm animals and unfamiliar spices – all mixed in together like an exotic aromatic soup. It was a far cry from the crazy congestion of the city.

Luis waited for them in the four-wheel drive, tapping his fingers impatiently on the steering wheel. He was anxious to get them down to Panajachel as quickly as possible and then head back to Guatemala City. It was all work as far as he was concerned. Once he had deposited them safely in one of the *hospedajes* beside the lake his assignment would be complete.

On the twisting road winding down to Panajachel they caught their first glimpse of Lake Atitlán. Emerging from the dense pine forest that blanketed the steep incline, they could suddenly see three majestic volcanoes on the far side of the vast shimmering lake. Flavia tugged on James' arm and beamed an enthusiastic smile at him. It had all been worthwhile. They had made the right decision. It was good that they had come. There was magic to be found here, after all.

They enquired unsuccessfully at several of the more obvious hotels along the main road into town but eventually found accommodation in a small two-storey dwelling on Calle Valencia. Tucked away behind the markets near the mouth of Rio Panajachel, Casa Hernández could accommodate five guests and had three rooms available for the night. Casa Hernández was a simple brick and stucco building daubed in streaky whitewash, with black wrought iron balconies on the upper level. Small rainbows and the figure of a Mayan woman carrying a basket of corn had been painted in gaudy colours beside the main

123

entrance.

Carmelita, an elderly woman with grey-black hair and dark enquiring eyes, was standing near the front door. Behind her in the small reception area, prominently displayed on a wooden shelf, were a number of painted figurines of Roman Catholic saints, all of them decorated with colourful fragments of Mayan hand-woven cloth. An ornate golden crucifix was mounted on the wall.

After greeting James and Flavia at the door Carmelita invited them to come inside and have a quick look upstairs. The rooms were all simply laid out and freshly painted in pastel yellow and white, with blue decorative motifs around the door. Each room had a single bed, a small wooden table, two wooden chairs and a bedside lamp. The bathrooms were clean, and there were hot water showers as well...

'It's around five American dollars a night for each room!,' said Flavia enthusiatically, translating the local currency. 'Shall we take them...?'

James replied with a spirited nod. The rooms looked fine. Casa Hernández was also close to the lake, close to the markets, and tucked away just a block or two from the main thoroughfare... a perfect location.

They hurried back downstairs to get their bags from the back of Luis' wagon. Flavia signed the paperwork the driver had brought with him and collected the mobile phone... for emergencies, just in case ('I'll only call you if I really have to...'). Then they trudged back up to their rooms, grateful it had all worked out so well.

Flavia thought the painted figurines and crucifix were a good omen. If Carmelita was really devout she would certainly be familiar with all the Catholic missions scattered around the lake.

Later that night, as they were eagerly devouring a welcome plate of corn and chicken tortillas, Flavia asked Carmelita to join them at their table. Then she began speaking to her in Spanish to make things a little easier.

'She says there are Catholic missions in most of the main towns near here,' said Flavia, translating slowly, sentence by sentence.

'In Sololá and Santiago, up north in Chichicastenango, and of course in Panajachel ...'

'Any others?' asked James

'She says there's also one in a little town called Xocomil, but it's harder to get to. Away from where the tourists go, off the main track...'

James asked Flavia to translate.

'It's called Xocomil, *Shocomil*... Mayan names starting with an "x" begin with a Shhhh....'

She pursed her lips to emphasize the effect.

James thought she looked cute doing that. He'd have to ask her to translate more often.

Flavia turned back to Carmelita and began speaking in Spanish once again. Soon Flavia was nodding her head enthusiastically, absorbing every small detail the old lady was telling her. 'She says we will need to get one of the local buses. They only leave once a day, up on Calle Real at the junction with Calle Santander. The mission is run by a priest called Pedro Delgado. She says he's a good man, a dedicated man, a true man of God. He's been there many years. She says he always helps the Mayan people, he holds healing services and he helps the poor. His wife used to be there with him, helping as well, but she died from chicken-pox many years ago when she was still a young woman...'

Flavia thanked her and looked back across the table. James had begun sipping from a large bowl of turtle soup.

She could rest more easily now. This was definitely a real breakthrough. Carmelita was obviously an inexhaustible source of local information. There had been no need to panic in Guatemala City, if panic was the right word for it. Here all you had to do was mention a name and everything just fell into place. Out here in Panajachel everyone knew everyone else and they probably knew everyone's private business as well, just for good measure.

'I've just realised that the prices here are all in quetzals,' said James, in between mouthfuls. He hadn't noticed up till now, because Flavia had been given the task of administering Uncle Conrad's money.

'It's the national icon, their sacred bird,' said Flavia. 'You'll find quetzals everywhere you look...'

'Obviously that's how they got into my dreams,' he said flippantly. He was beginning to enjoy himself. He liked it here. He was beginning to relax, take things easy. And the soup tasted really superb.

After their meal they went upstairs to unpack. Later James knocked on Flavia's door. Could he come in for a moment? There was something he wanted to ask her...

Flavia viewed him suspiciously as he sat down beside her on the bed. It was a professional trip, she reminded him again. Just because they were away together in a sweet little hotel beside a lake in Guatemala didn't mean that James could take advantage...

'Don't worry,' he said, reassuring her. 'Remember, I work in an office full of women. I know all about personal boundaries...'

She smiled, a little embarrassed. Obviously she had misjudged him.

'I wanted to ask you about something else, something quite different...,' he continued. ' ...about magic and the local shaman traditions and all the things Uncle Conrad asked us to investigate. Does the sort of magic you were studying at the castle connect with anything we're likely to discover over here?'

'Good question...' she replied. 'but right now I really don't know. Coming to Guatemala is new for me as well...'

But James wanted to probe a little deeper. He wanted to get some sort of insight into how much she really knew...

'Just before Uncle Conrad suggested sending us out here, I had a meeting with him in Brighton....in the park, near the Royal Pavilion. There wasn't anyone else around. He said he would show me how he could use magic to change his appearance. How he could transform into a figure from ancient mythology...'

James was watching for Flavia's response but right now she wasn't giving anything away. He continued with what he wanted to say.

'Then he did something amazing, right there in front of me. He changed into the form of an ancient Egyptian god, with a human body and the head of an ibis...'

'Thoth...,' said Flavia emphatically in her most direct matter-of-fact manner, as if there was nothing to it at all. 'Thoth...the ancient Egyptian god of wisdom. He's one of Uncle Conrad's favourites. He does it all the time...'

'Really?'

'Well, not all the time. But quite often...'

She paused for a moment, wondering whether James was seriously interested or just stringing her along. But she could see now that he was genuinely curious.

'It's called shapeshifting. You focus your willpower on changing your body image. You make a conscious shift by creating a thought-form in your imagination...'

A thought-form? Imagination...?

Flavia made it all sound so easy, so straightforward. James was sure it was much more difficult than that.

'Can you do it too?' he asked.

'I can,' she said, 'but I sometimes I take a little longer. I haven't been practising as long as Uncle Conrad. He's been shapeshifting for years...'

Flavia could see from his expression that James was expecting a demonstration.

'Go over there and sit down on the floor,' she told him. 'I'll need some space around me so I can relax and concentrate. But

I'll try to do it so you can see for yourself. Stay really quiet and still. To make it happen you have to build up your willpower, step by step, and it's easy to get distracted...'

She closed her eyes, straightened her back and began to inhale and exhale in long, measured breaths. Soon she had slowed her breathing right down so it was barely audible. Then she became suddenly very quiet and still. She seemed to be entering some sort of trance...

Meanwhile James was feasting his eyes on her, watching her intently, soaking in every drop of her exotic Latin soul. He loved her long dark eyelashes, the solitary brown freckle on one side of her chin, the small dimples in her cheeks. She really was a lovely young woman. It was great just to be with her, to have her all to himself here in Panajachel...

But then something began to change.

Furrowed lines began to appear across Flavia's brow. Her cheeks became fuller, her skin more weathered. And her body seemed to be filling out as well. She was becoming more buxom, more motherly.

She's no longer a lithe young woman, he thought. She's lost the sweet bloom of youth and she's moved gracefully into middle age. She's taken on the persona of a middle-aged woman...

And then she changed again...

Now she was shrinking down by stages. Becoming more wrinkled, withdrawing into herself. Allowing the years to take their toll and leave their markings etched into her skin. Her face was becoming increasingly more lined, her smile irregular. Her hair had become stiff and wiry. It turned grey and then white...

Suddenly she was a shrivelled old woman, a grandmother, a wise old crone...a figure out of Macbeth....the sort of haggard witch who would make your hair stand up on end and frighten you to half to death if you met her alone on a windswept moor...

James was amazed, intrigued. This was the other side of Flavia, the magical side she hadn't shown him before. The other side she had only hinted at...

Then, just like Sir Conrad in the park in Brighton, Flavia suddenly reversed the process of transformation. From being a haggard old witch she slowly reverted to being a middle-aged woman before gradually changing back into her beautiful, exotic self....the enticing young woman James knew he was already in love with.

'Fantastic. Really fantastic...'

He could barely contain his amazement.

'That was shapeshifting through the different phases of being a woman,' said Flavia almost casually. ' Maiden, mother, crone...'

'How did you do it? How did you manage to put yourself through all those amazing changes...'

Flavia was suddenly evasive, back to her mysterious and elusive persona.

'Practice,' she said finally, '...just practice. I'm sure you could master shapeshifting too, if you really put your mind to it...'

James wasn't so sure. He always thought of himself as just a regular sort of guy. A journalist, a celebrity feature writer. He was really just tipping his toe in the water with all this magic. The castle, and everything associated with it, had been a real revelation. It was all new to him, and very much outside his normal range of experience...

'I think one magician in the touring party is quite sufficient for the moment,' he said breezily. '...but I'm very impressed...'

He paused for a moment and then decided to tell her.

'...But I want you to know that I think you're a very special person. You're different from any other woman I've ever met. You're very special to me, even if this is just a professional business trip....'

She blushed a little. It was the first time he had seen her do that. He went up and put his warm hand on hers. Then he kissed her gently on the cheek.

'Goodnight,' he said. 'Sweet dreams...'

129

He walked over to the door, slipped through, and half-closed it behind him.

Then he looked back in with a cheeky smile, just before leaving.

'...and it was great watching you dissolve your personal boundaries...'

Later that night he lay in his bed looking up at the ceiling trying hard to invoke the special, erotic dreams he had been so fond of in the past. He tried to imagine himself playing tennis with Flavia. Naked tennis, with their bodies moving elegantly from one side of the court to the other.... He wanted to imagine Flavia like this, to really see her pristine, naked beauty. But the dreams refused to come, despite his best intentions.

Instead he dreamt of quetzal birds, rainbows and an old Mayan woman carrying a basket of corn. His dreams were painted in gaudy colours, just like the mural beside the entrance to the hotel.

21

NEXT DAY AFTER BREAKFAST they wandered casually through the markets, sifting through piles of hand-woven fabrics and clusters of assorted woodcarvings, just for something to do. The red and yellow ex-American schoolbus to Xocomil would come through town around midday so there was still a bit of time to fill in. They sauntered down to the lake and gazed out at the view, which was really amazing. But Panajachel itself was nothing to write home about... a rambling settlement sprawling haphazardly around the foreshore. There were plenty of exotic Mayan handicrafts to admire but the place itself looked makeshift, almost as if it had happened by accident because of its superb location. They quickly realised that westerners had been drifting through here for years. Even the hippies had got there before them — their hand-painted Volkwagen vans were very much in evidence down beside the lake. And there were numerous European tourists strolling around the dusty streets as well. Many of them could be seen scouring the markets for photo opportunities or practising *buenos días* and *muchas gracias* with the Spanish-speaking vendors to show their respect for local etiquette.

Around thirty minutes before the bus was due Flavia and James started walking slowly back along Calle Santander towards the junction with Calle Real. They found the bus-stop beside a small shop that sold earthenware pots and hand-painted ceramic tiles, its stucco walls festooned with bright decorations and wavy, curling writing.

A small crowd of people had begun to gather around the bus-stop: a cluster of amiable middle-aged men with neatly trussed bundles of wood and several boxes of melons... an eye-catching group of Mayan mothers dressed in colourful shawls and blouses, clinging desperately to their small children to stop them running out onto the street...... two young women carrying bundles of freshly cut flowers in green plastic buckets... and an old man with a feisty black hen in a rustic wooden cage...

Then they could see the old red and yellow schoolbus grinding laboriously towards them through a thick cloud of dust. They scrambled on board and Flavia thrust a few quetzales into the hands of the driver. It didn't cost much to get to Xocomil but the bus was almost full already. They struggled with their suitcases and found two separate seats down towards the back.

James wedged himself in between two village workers carrying shovels and a variety of farm implements and Flavia nestled in beside an overweight olive-skinned woman wearing a white mesh shawl and a black cotton dress. She was carrying a large basket of groceries that she had hoisted up onto her knee. She didn't look very comfortable but then no-one else did either. It was probably always like this, thought Flavia, but at least they were now on their way to Xocomil, and the trip couldn't last forever. With a bit of luck they would be there in an around an hour. At least, that's what Carmelita had told her in Panajachel just before they left...

Soon the bus was making its way out of the main township and heading west along a dirt road. Then it began climbing slowly away from the lake. The road itself was narrow and precarious. There were numerous potholes in the coarse gravel surface, and the bus had to lurch regularly from one side to the other in order to avoid them. Fortunately there was little traffic coming from the opposite direction.

As the bus struggled with its load through the narrow mountain passes, Flavia looked back towards the lake. But there was really no point at all. Clouds of dust billowed up into the air behind them and it was impossible to see anything clearly. The windows of the old schoolbus were scratched and smeared with streaks of dirt but every now and then she glimpsed stretches of fertile open country that looked exotic and inviting. From time to time the bus eased its way past dense clusters of overhanging palm trees and not far from Xocomil they skirted a coffee plantation with its trees laid out in neat rows. Responding to Flavia's obvious interest in the local terrain the olive-skinned woman in the black dress broke her silence and spoke to her in Spanish.

'¡El café está muy bueno!' ... the locals around here say the coffee grown in Guatemala is the best in the world...

Finally the old schoolbus started to descend through a narrow pass, its brakes screeching angrily as it lunged precariously close to the irregular gulleys on either side of the road. Rising cautiously from her seat to peer past the driver, Flavia could make out the shape of a colonial Spanish church spire in the distance. Then further details came gradually into view: the colourful markets lining the main street, the large open courtyard beside the church, clusters of small stuccoed buildings adjoining the city square, and sections of kerbside fencing reinforced by sheets of painted corrugated iron. An enthusiastic crowd of people and several barking dogs had gathered to meet them in the main square.

With a shudder the bus ground finally to a halt and quickly began disgorging its bustling passengers. Dazed and weary from their trip, James and Flavia struggled from the bus with their heavy suitcases and found themselves standing in the main city square. They looked around and walked slowly across to a vacant wooden bench. For the moment it felt good just to be here — time to take a short break and get their bearings. After they had rested for a little while, they could walk down into the town centre and look for somewhere to stay.

Later they strolled down beside the old church. It was an impressive colonial structure with a tall bell-tower, elegant brick pattern-work and ornamental flourishes around the arches. The whitewashed walls had begun to crumble in different places but there was still a certain grandeur that spoke of earlier, more prosperous times. A robust wooden door with heavy metal fittings marked the main entrance to the building and a smaller door was open at the side of the church for parishioners and visitors. Flavia looked across at the small stone plaque embedded in the wall beside the main entrance. It read *Iglesia de Santo Tomás, 1542*. The church must have built soon after the Spanish conquered Guatemala, thought Flavia reflectively. It was obviously the most distinctive building in town and there weren't any other old colonial structures around the central square except for the large ornate fountain in the forecourt. Maybe earthquakes had ravaged Xocomil at an earlier time or other competing towns had expanded more rapidly under Spanish rule... it would be good to find out more about the history of the place.

After leaving the church they strolled past the market-place in the direction of the lake. Flavia was already feeling very much at home. She liked it much more than Panajachel and it had been well worth the effort to get here.

Not far from the marketplace, down on Calle Ramos, they came across a small *hospedaje* called Mama Rosalinda's. Set back slightly from the street, it was painted in slaked pale pink and had little pots of bright red geraniums clustered around the entrance. A large jolly woman with curly black hair was watering the flowers and looked up as they strolled by.

'*¡Hola!*' she called out as they drew closer.'*¿Buscan alojamiento dos habitaciones?'*

Flavia asked if they could look inside. The location was close to the church and marketplace and seemed ideal. Once again she and James made a hasty inspection upstairs. The rooms were similar to those in Panajachel, with single beds, simple wooden furniture and very welcome hot water, as before.

And the rate was even cheaper. Only 35 quetzales a night, a little over four American dollars for each room!

They hauled their suitcases upstairs and collapsed onto the pristine beds. At last they were here in Xocomil with a roof over their heads! In a sense their journey was just beginning. They agreed to meet downstairs in an hour and then go for a walk around the town.

When James came down to join Flavia she was already sitting beside a large wooden table, deep in conversation with Mama Rosalinda herself.

'I've been finding out all about Xocomil,' she said as he sat down next to her. '...what goes on here, what makes the place tick...'

'And...?'

'Looks like one of the big drawcards here is the healing service at Santo Tomás. Every Sunday scores of people come here, just for laying on of hands, or to hear the sermons of Father Delgado...'

James nodded receptively as Flavia continued.

'Mayan people, Hispanics, visitors... Rosalinda says everyone is welcome at the church. Most of the people staying here at this hotel have come to town just to attend the healing services....'

Mama Rosalinda had a huge, expansive smile to accompany her more than ample figure. She seemed to smile whenever there was an exchange of conversation, regardless of what was being said. But one thing was certain, she knew how to make her guests feel welcome. If they got back by dark a big plate of spicy chicken and vegetables would be waiting for them on the table, together with soup and cornbread if they wanted it....

James and Flavia thanked her and promised to return by nightfall. It would be good to spend what remained of the afternoon just wandering around the town and strolling down beside the lake. They walked out into the cobbled pathway of Calle Ramos and headed down towards the water. Several of the smaller shops had already begun to close for the day, pulling down their shutters as ever- lengthening shadows fell across the narrow streets. Here and there children still darted around amusing themselves with their games, and from time to time locals trundled by carrying bundles of wood and domestic produce. Xocomil was much quieter than Panajachel and well off the tourist route.

James and Flavia decided they liked it that way. Here they could just immerse themselves in what was happening around them and enter into the spirit of the place. Hopefully, too, they would be able to track down the local shamans and find out more about the curious biblical text that had surfaced at the Mission...

They walked down to the edge of the lake, making their way past the dugout canoes that had been drawn up onto the sand. A gentle breeze was sweeping in off the water as they paused to look out at Lake Atitlán. The water was now a deep azure blue and in the distance three magnificent volcanoes marked the edge of the vast expanse.

They both felt it at the same time. There was a mystery and an allure out there beyond the lake that had risen from a world of magical awakening.

This was a place of dreams and visions... a land of spirits and ancient, forgotten gods. And it was a place, too, that had many timeless stories to tell. Soon, they felt sure, it would open its heart and yield up its secrets....secrets they could share if they were willing to receive them.

22

WHEN THEY ARRIVED at the church on Sunday morning more than half of the aisles were already full. Many of the visitors were frail and elderly women but in some instances it seemed that whole families had come, squeezing in together to make room in the crowded wooden pews. Some of the women were dressed in colourful *huipiles*, others in simple working clothes. A group of young children sat playing on the reed mat floor.

Flavia glanced around the church. The walls were fashioned in flaking white plaster and the arched ceiling was supported by robust wooden beams. Numerous figurines of saints adorned the walls, many of them decorated with pieces of ornamental Mayan fabric. Generous offerings of food and flowers were clustered on the ground in front of the altar. A large sculpted figure of the crucified Christ was mounted on the wall towards the front of the church. The altar itself was a simple brass cross that glinted as soft beams of light filtered in through the windows.

The officiating priest, Father Pedro Delgado, made his way to the front and welcomed them all to the church and its healing mission. The service began with prayers and then a number of hymns that Flavia didn't recognize even though she could follow most of the Spanish phrasing. James just sat there taking it all in, closing his eyes from time to time to let the heartfelt singing waft over him like a gentle breeze.

Later several members of the audience went forward to receive healing blessings from the priest. Placing his hands on their heads and shoulders, Father Delgado prayed for an end to all the fears and anxieties that tormented their troubled souls, and for health and strength to return to their frail and aching bodies. He was obviously a deeply compassionate and caring man, thought Flavia, as she watched him ministering to their needs. He was clearly someone who carried on his shoulders the hopes and aspirations of entire families within the extended community. His whole approach was both simple and direct. He was there to help the poor and elderly. He was there to spread a message of healing and goodwill among the local people.

At the end of the service, after most of the parishioners had dispersed, Flavia and James went up to introduce themselves. Pedro brushed his hair back out of his eyes and shook hands with both of them in turn. He was pleased to welcome them, he had noticed them in the crowd. Were they just passing through or were they hoping to stay for a while?

'Well, we were hoping we might get a chance to meet up with you, ask your opinion about a few things,' said Flavia, speaking first in Spanish and then more slowly in English. 'If you've got the time...'

'I can speak a little in English if that makes things easier,' said Pedro, taking care with his phrasing. 'I learnt it when I was still at college in Barcelona... I can remember a few words and expressions...'

'You are Spanish originally...?'

He nodded.

'I was born in Spain but I came here many years ago, once I had completed my training for the priesthood. I have spent almost my whole life here. Here in Xocomil, and in other towns around the lake...'

He paused for a moment and looked down at his watch.

'Maybe you would like to come round to the back of the church a little later?' he asked. 'My house is just around there...'

He pointed with an outstretched hand.

'...just past the fountain and through the garden. You'll see it there. It's good to see some new faces here in town... Maybe I can help you in some way..?'

They agreed to come back in half an hour, after he had had time to tidy up and put a few things away. James and Flavia smiled knowingly at each other. Things were working out just fine. It seemed to be really easy to make the right connections here in Xocomil. It was such a small place that everyone watched out for everyone else.

Later they made their way round to the back of the church and found Father Delgado sitting on a wooden chair on his verandah, beside a flowering hibiscus tree. He had changed into an old T-shirt and jeans and was leaning back against a cushion.

He waved and got up from his chair as they walked across to join him.

'Please call me Pedro,' he said, 'Everyone calls me Pedro...it's not so formal...'

Then they went and sat down around a table on the verandah. This is perfect, thought Flavia to herself, really perfect....With a bit of luck they would have an opportunity to ask him about the things that had actually brought them here...

But she had to remind herself to take things one step at a time. Don't rush in, she told herself. Take it easy... take it at the local pace. She smiled and nodded graciously as Pedro offered them a cool drink.

'I guess you could say I'm a spiritual seeker,' said Flavia once Pedro had returned to the table. '...and James is a writer for a local newspaper. We're both from England... this is our first visit to Guatemala...'

'And your first visit to Xocomil...?'

'Yes, our first visit to Xocomil...'

'Well, Xocomil is a special place,' said Pedro, stroking his chin. 'Xocomil is the sort of town you come to if you're looking for something...'

He took a sip from his glass.

'Xocomil is a little off the beaten track. Usually there are particular reasons why people come here...'

'James and I are both very interested in the local spiritual traditions,' said Flavia, seizing the moment. 'We are fascinated by the Mayan culture, and intrigued by the way it ties in with

Christian belief. Here in your church the two traditions seem to weave in so easily, so effortlessly...'

Pedro seemed to agree. He nodded and asked her to continue.

'We wanted to ask you about the local legends. About Santo Tomás coming to Central America... and the stories about Kukulcan..'

'Ah,' said Pedro. 'So that is why you have come...'

He paused for a moment and Flavia wondered whether she had already dived in too deep.

'Well, certainly there are stories...legends...'

His face broke into an ironic smile.

'...but who can say whether they are really true?'

Flavia felt she had to probe a little deeper.

'What do you think yourself?' she asked. 'Do you think they are really true...?'

'Well,' he said, 'I don't know how much you already know. But the local Mayan legends speak of a spiritual teacher who came here many, many years ago. Perhaps in the lifetime of Jesus, or soon afterwards. He came in a large wooden boat from across the sea and arrived here on the western shore. He had a pale skin and a dark brown beard. Somehow — we don't know how — the local people understood what he was telling them. He spoke of love and peace, and urged an end to blood sacrifice. This was a message they hadn't heard before...'

'Could this have been Jesus?' asked Flavia. For the moment she was just anxious to draw out what he knew.

'No, not Jesus himself... No, I don't believe that....'

He paused and then continued.

'...but maybe one of his disciples...'

'And who would be the most likely?' asked Flavia. She was really fascinated to know whether Father Delgado had come to the same conclusion as Uncle Conrad.

'Well, most likely it was Didymos Judas Thomas,' said Pedro. 'In our scriptures he is referred to as Jesus' twin brother. The name Didymos actually means "twin"...'

'But is it really possible that he could have travelled all the way to Central America?' asked Flavia. On the face of it, it all sounded so far-fetched...

'I agree, it does seem rather unlikely when you first consider it,' said Pedro, choosing his words carefully. 'But we know that Didymos Judas Thomas went to southern India. He was one of the first disciples and we know he travelled widely, more than most of the other disciples. Sometimes he is called "The Disciple of the East". He took the teachings of Jesus to India and he founded the church of Saint Thomas in Kerala... his followers are still there to this day....'

Pedro looked across at Flavia. There was more he could tell her. Did she want him to continue?

She nodded eagerly. She very much wanted to hear what he had to say...

'There were fine boat builders in that part of India... builders who could construct large wooden boats. Maybe Saint Thomas Didymos continued with his travels after he left India. Maybe he came here by boat and landed in Guatemala...'

And the Mayans knew him as Santo Tomás...?'

'No, of course not,' said Pedro, responding to her question.

'He was only recognised as Santo Tomás much later on. After the Spanish conquistadors arrived....after they had conquered the country. The Mayans knew Saint Thomas by another name. They called him Kukulcan...'

'So could Santo Tomás and Kukulcan really be one and the same...?'

'To tell you the truth I do think it is possible,' said Pedro. 'No, actually, it is more than possible. I now think it is very likely...'

'Have you changed your mind...?'

'Well, we have just found something, here in Guatemala. Something which has taken us a little by surprise....'

Flavia was listening intently, absorbing every word.

'I have had a friend staying with me for a while... a colleague from overseas. He is an expert in these things. He will be here later this afternoon. Maybe if you would like to come back later you can ask him yourself...'

* * *

Towards the end of the afternoon James and Flavia made their way back across the paved market square and walked round to the back of the church. They could see Pedro standing in the garden. He had cut some yellow hibiscus blooms and was placing them in an earthenware vase.

They walked over to the verandah together.

'I've been expecting you. Mario will be here soon...'

'Mario?' asked Flavia.

'My colleague, Mario Burri. He's a biblical scholar from the Vatican...'

Pedro went off to get some cool fruit juice. When he got back it was obvious there were other things he wanted to say.

'You know, there are some other points I forgot to mention earlier, things which are maybe more than a coincidence...'

He sat down and took a sip of cool, refreshing juice.

'The Mayan people have a famous calendar wheel. No doubt you have heard of it. For over five thousand years it has marked the passage of time...'

Flavia and James nodded. They had heard of the calendar wheel from Uncle Conrad but only had a rudimentary under-standing...

'The Mayans say that the world as we know it will come to an end on the 21st of December, 2012. But they also say that from that day onwards the world will begin to transform in a positive and spiritual way. So 21st December 2012 marks the beginning of something completely and radically new...the beginning of heaven on earth...'

For the moment Flavia and James were speechless. They looked across at each other in amazement. Was this the date of the Second Coming ? Maybe Uncle Conrad had been right after all...

But Pedro had still more to tell them.

'And here's an intriguing coincidence...' said Pedro, taking a quick sip of juice from his glass.

'The festival of Santo Tomás is celebrated each and every year here in Guatemala. It has been that way for as long as anyone can remember. Perhaps you can guess when the festival of Santo Tomás reaches its high point?'

Pedro didn't wait for them to answer his question.

'On 21st December... on the same day that the Mayan calendar wheel comes to a close in 2012...'

He put down his glass.

'Now that's a fascinating coincidence, wouldn't you agree...?'

Their conversation was interrupted by the arrival of a short, intense-looking man in a grey suit. He seemed short of breath and was obviously very much in need of a cool drink. Pedro urged him to take off his jacket and relax a little. This wasn't the Vatican after all...

'Mario Burri...' said the short man in the grey suit, extending his hand to introduce himself.

'Flavia and James have just arrived from England,' said Pedro, draping his friend's jacket over a chair. 'They got into Xocomil a few days ago and came to the healing service this morning. We've been talking about Santo Tomás and Kukulcan, and the end of the Mayan calendar wheel in 2012. I told them about your biblical research...'

Mario Burri looked suddenly nervous.

'Did you mention the discovery?' he asked.

'No, I thought you might like to tell them yourself...'

'Well, I'm not sure I should say too much at this stage. I would need to get clearance from the Vatican...'

Flavia was intrigued but James had already sensed what he was alluding to.

'We found an old document here in Guatemala,' said Mario Burri cautiously. He seemed suddenly uncomfortable knowing Pedro had even mentioned their discovery.

'It's some sort of biblical text. My job has been to translate it and evaluate its significance...'

'And what have you found?' asked Flavia, anxious to tease out more information.

'Well, the document itself purports to be about the Second Coming,' said Mario Burri without elaborating. '... but there are lots of apocalyptic texts like that from every period of history. In the Middle Ages there was a popular market for end-of-the-world prophecies. People simply thrived on them. With tragedies like the Black Death ravaging Europe the commonfolk hoped for the best but expected the worst. But I was asked to come out here and take a look for myself. I've already completed the translation and sent it back to Rome...'

'And do you think it really is significant?' asked Flavia, persisting with her questions.

'No I don't, actually,' he replied. 'It's an interesting curiosity...probably just another forgery. In all likelihood it dates back around the time of Alvarado and the Spanish conquest of Guatemala. But there's nothing in it that we need to take seriously, nothing we should pay any attention to...'

He seemed suddenly defensive as he sat eyeing Flavia across the table, sipping intensely on his cool drink.

That was probably all she would get out of him for the moment. Something told her he wanted to nip this conversation right in the bud as soon as possible.

23

AS THEY WALKED BACK to Mama Rosalinda's James and Flavia both agreed that Mario Burri seemed to have something to hide, that he hadn't been completely forthcoming about what he had discovered. But for the moment they decided to let the matter rest. Pedro seemed more open and honest with what he believed. And he had said he was willing to help them. Maybe he could introduce them to some shamans in the local community... help them get a taste of the magic and mystery surrounding Lake Atitlán...

Next day they went round to see if Pedro was home. Once again they found him digging in his garden at the back of the church. He glanced up as they walked over to greet him.

'Hello once again,' said Flavia amiably, '...and thanks for introducing us to Mario Burri. What he had to say was really fascinating...'

Pedro placed the plant he had been potting in a secure position beneath the hibiscus tree. Then he looked up so he could pay closer attention.

'We were wondering if we could ask just one more favour...We were hoping you might know some of the local shamans who live around Xocomil... local people who still follow the old spiritual traditions....?'

He pondered for a moment, stroking the patch of grey stubble on his chin.

There was Arana and his sister, but he didn't really know them very well. He had enjoyed the occasional sociable banter with the old man, Nachancan, when he was still alive. And now, of course, Itzamna had come across and embraced the Christian faith. But then there was the mother...

'There used to be a well- known and highly- regarded shaman who lived up behind the town in a small family compound,' said

Pedro after thinking about it for a while. 'Sadly he is no longer with us... he died a short while ago.... but his wife, Zafrina, comes down here to the markets most mornings. She sells fruit and vegetables and also lengths of cloth that she weaves on her loom. I could introduce you to her ...'

Flavia and James nodded eagerly. It would be wonderful to meet her...

'You'll have to speak slowly, in fairly basic Spanish,' said Pedro. 'That's not being unkind, it's just how it is... Most of the older Mayan folk around here speak a little bit of Spanish but they prefer to speak to each other in their own local dialects...'

He could see that James and Flavia were really keen to immerse themselves in the local spiritual traditions but he wondered how they would bridge the obvious cultural gulf. It was one thing to be keen, quite another to communicate effectively.

'I speak a little bit of Spanish as well,' said Flavia quickly, downplaying her professional role as a translator back home, '... hopefully enough to get by...'

They agreed to meet early next day, down in the marketplace across from the church. Pedro would introduce them to Zafrina and they could take it from there. Maybe she in turn would take them to meet Arana and Malinali, but he couldn't make any promises. The local people around here take you as they find you, he told them. If they like you and respond to the spirit of who you are and how you come across to them, then doors may begin to open. But if not, they will never invite you into their world and those doors will remain closed forever...

When they arrived at the marketplace Pedro was already deep in conversation with Zafrina. Today she had brought down a pile of woven *huipiles* and a basket containing squash, pumpkins, chillies and freshly cut corn. Then she had spread out a blanket in her usual place beside the steps on the paved market square. Pedro had already told her that there were two young people from England who would like to meet her... spiritual seekers who were keen to learn more about the ways of the Maya. They seemed to know a little about the path of the shaman but they wanted to know more. Would she be willing to talk with them about that?

'Ah, there you are,' said Pedro as he saw Flavia and James wending their way through the crowded market stalls. 'Zafrina is here and I am sure you will enjoy speaking with her.'

And Zafrina, in turn, seemed pleased to meet them. Pedro had already told her that Flavia would speak with her in Spanish. They could take it just a few words at a time... she was happy to answer a few questions and see if she could be of assistance. Meanwhile Pedro had some matters he had to attend to. He would leave them now just to talk and spend a little time together. He would be back at the church later in the day if they needed him for anything else...

Flavia smiled and sat down on the blanket beside Zafrina. Instinctively the older woman reached for her young companion's hand and clasped it tightly as she looked deep into her eyes. Flavia felt suddenly exposed and vulnerable. There was something very powerful in this intimate, eye-to-eye contact as if the old lady was searching her soul, reaching in where no-one had ever reached before...

And yet there was also something about her that was welcoming and receptive, a feeling that went way beyond any sense of scrutiny and invasion. There was a real warmth about Zafrina, a sense of openness that suggested in the long run they could get closer to each other by honestly expressing their intentions. Flavia felt suddenly confident that this would all work out fine...that this was just the local Mayan way for two total strangers to get to know each other a little better...

Already she felt more relaxed. As she eased her way gradually into more general conversation, she began to explain in Spanish why she and James had come over to Guatemala.

147

How they valued the spiritual ways of the Mayan people....How they were both drawn to the path of the shaman and wished to learn more about it in any way possible... How they were personally attuned not so much to conventional forms of religious practice but instead to the powerful and mysterious forces of Nature...

And all the while as they sat there together beside the market steps Zafrina seemed happy just to listen to her, nodding and occasionally smiling in response. Soon Flavia began to wonder whether what she had been saying sounded just like a bunch of simple platitudes. Was the old lady smiling because this was all too absurd? Or was it just way over her head?

But maybe there was another reason. Maybe Flavia's way of explaining things had actually struck home... showing that she and James had come to Guatemala with an open mind and a receptive spirit...

Then, in a flash of certainty, she had her answer. When Zafrina squeezed her hand and looked once more into her eyes, Flavia knew that she had truly been heard. That Zafrina really had understood... that in some mysterious way this had been more like a coming together of kindred souls whose paths had now crossed....

Speaking in simple halting Spanish, Zafrina asked Flavia if she and James would like to come and meet her children. It was her son, Arana, and her daughter, Malinali, who were now the custodians for the shaman path following the recent death of her husband. Would they like to come at the end of the day tomorrow so they could all walk back to the house together? Then they could talk about these things more freely. There would be many things they could share and discuss. And besides, she added, her children could speak with them in English since they had spent some time as students in New Mexico... in Taos and Albuquerque. For them the language wouldn't be a problem...

Flavia was thrilled by Zafrina's warm and positive response.

She grabbed James by the arm.

'This is really great !' she said excitedly. 'We can go home with Zafrina tomorrow night. We'll get a chance to meet her children, Arana and Malinali. We'll be able to get a sense of whether the old magic is still alive...'

James could see she was really delighted. Her whole face was glowing with enthusiasm.

She turned back to Zafrina, and offered her hand once again.

'Thankyou, so much...' she said, once again in Spanish.'*Gracias...muchas gracias...*' She and James would come back tomorrow and meet her here in the marketplace, around five in the afternoon. Then they could take it from there...

24

NEXT DAY FLAVIA AND JAMES brought Zafrina a large bunch of yellow and purple flowers. When Zafrina saw them her crinkled face broke into a broad smile as she held out her hand to greet them both. Then she quickly gathered what remained of the produce she had brought down to the market, slung the remaining unsold lengths of fabric across her shoulder and got ready to leave.

Slowly they made their way along the rocky track that led back up the mountain, Zafrina balancing her basket skilfully on her head. Glancing back behind them, Flavia could see the little settlement of Xocomil nestling neatly on the small stretch of inhabitable land between the mountain and the lake. The colonial church bell-tower was clearly the most distinctive feature and marked the very centre of the town. A few houses lay in small clusters along the foreshore. She could see now that where she and James were staying, at Mama Rosalinda's, was close to the very heart of Xocomil.

Soon they had reached the rough-hewn stone wall that marked the edge of the family compound. They stopped for a moment to take in the view. The expanse of Lake Atitlán was truly inspiring, a wash of deep blue edged by three majestic volcanoes whose steep slopes plunged straight into the vast and awesome depths.

Zafrina watched them closely as they gazed out across the tranquil waters.

'That's the home of the Lake Mother,' she said to Flavia, speaking slowly in Spanish with a cheeky grin on her face. 'Today she has calmed the waters... to show that you are welcome...'

Flavia beamed back at her. It was great that the old lady had a sense of humour as well...

They made their way along a narrow track that led through dense bushes and tall grass and past a rickety wire fence that was straining to contain the shrubbery. Finally they could see the distinctive outline of the thatch and stucco huts, hidden partly by a cluster of flowering shrubs and large, expansive palm trees whose broad fronds drooped down across the path. Brushing aside the palms with her arm, Zafrina called out to Arana and Malinali to let them know she had arrived.

Arana and Malinali were standing in the doorway to welcome them all home.

After being introduced by their mother, Arana led James and Flavia into the main room and invited them to sit down on the woollen rugs strewn across the floor. Large wax candles had been lit around the room, casting flickering shadows across the white stucco walls.

The room itself was simple and unadorned, with dense roof-thatching and wooden beams overhead. The dirt floor had been covered with a scattering of reed mats and colourful woollen rugs, the dazzling array of deep reds and purples adding colour to the undecorated room.

Two large earthenware pots containing soup and an exotic vegetable brew were resting on the hearth, warmed by hot coals. Already the room had begun to fill with a rich mix of aromas, the appetising smell of hot bubbling vegetables blending in with the distinctive odour of wood-smoke.

Some short wooden stools were clustered around the hearth but for the moment James and Flavia found it more comfortable to sit on the rugs. It was good just to be here...good to finally catch a glimpse of a very different world...

When they had settled down, Malinali brought them cornbread and bowls of hot soup.

'I think our mother has already told you we can speak a little in English,' she said with a broad, cheerful smile. 'A few years ago Arana and I spent some time in the United States, on a cultural exchange programme. But we've got a bit rusty now, since we don't speak English so often with each other...'

'It's really great to be here,' said Flavia, taking the bowl in her hands.

'We're so pleased to meet you...and thankyou for your kindness. We were so fortunate to meet Zafrina down in the marketplace...'

The soup was tasty and full of unfamiliar flavours. James was already eagerly devouring it in large mouthfuls as Flavia started to explain what had brought them to Xocomil.

Expanding on what she had already told Zafrina, Flavia recounted yet again how she and James had come to Guatemala to try to meet the local shamans, that their spiritual path embraced the magic of Nature and the cosmos, that they had a sincere desire to make contact with the ancient ones...

But Malinali already seemed to know.

'We were expecting you,' she said finally, when Flavia had finished. 'You don't have to explain. We already knew that you were coming...'

Flavia put down her bowl so the soup wouldn't spill.

'You expected us...?'

Malinali glanced knowingly at her brother who was sitting beside her, and then looked back again at Flavia.

'I think we all know that this is an important time to honour the old ways, the sacred ways... but it is also a time for sharing, I sent a queztal helper-spirit to call you, to find you...and now you have come...'

Flavia was utterly speechless. She remembered how a queztal-bird had appeared in her visions during the drum journey back at the castle and how she had then passed it on to James as part of the healing. This was all quite extraordinary...

Arana felt he should expand on what his sister had been saying.

'Our father died just a short time ago. You may have heard

that he was highly regarded by our people... both as a shaman and as a leader...'

Flavia nodded. She and James had heard from many people that he was revered by the local community...

'Well, it has fallen to us to continue the ceremonial duties that members of our family have performed for endless generations...'

He glanced across at his sister and then paused to acknowledge his mother, who had joined them around the hearth.

'Malinali attends to the oracle and performs the women's ceremonies she has learnt from Zafrina...'

He looked across at Flavia and then in turn at James.

'... and I must perform the rituals of the Calendar Wheel and open the Path of Sacred Way. These are the duties I was given by my father...'

Arana seemed suddenly more serious, weighed down by the awesome responsibility of the tasks which lay ahead.

Malinali could sense the burden her brother was carrying but at the same time she hoped he would lighten up a little. She leaned across and urged him to finish his soup.

'It's all right,' she whispered encouragingly. 'It's all right. We're among friends now...'

Arana seemed to relax a little more. He sipped on his soup, put down his bowl, and continued with what he wanted to say.

'My father explained certain things to me. Some of those things must remain a secret but there are other things I can share with you...'

Flavia and James remained silent, listening attentively to every word.

'As I said, in the days ahead it has fallen to me to open the Path of the Sacred Way. This is a ceremony which honours our sacred Calendar Wheel. And there is a task connected with it which I must perform as well, and that is to honour Kukulcan...'

Flavia was intrigued. This was an unexpected connection, this crossing of the mystic paths... the amazing way in which spiritual powers of connection seemed to know no boundaries. And now she and James were privileged to be here at this special moment... at this special time.

'Is there any way we can be of service to you?' she asked.

'As Malinali explained,' said Arana, 'we knew that you were coming, we expected you here... In our ritual ceremony to Kukulcan we honour the great teacher who came among our people from far away across the ocean. You too have come to be with us from a distant land... from a place far from here. Our ceremony honours a sharing of the paths. But if you wish to assist us there is something we must agree on first...'

'And what is that?'

'Before you can be present in any of our ceremonies you must first be purified, cleansed... transformed into sacred vessels to honour the presence of the ancient ones... That is something that must be done before we can take this any further...'

Flavia glanced across at James. She felt suddenly nervous and uncertain. It was like venturing into completely unexplored territory...

'Don't worry. Nothing terrible will happen to you,' said Arana with a reassuring grin. '...but there are certain healing and cleansing procedures we must perform...'

'What do they involve?' asked James. He knew deep inside he would probably take the risk.

'You, James, would have to come with me. Alone, at night. Up on the mountain. You will be cleansed and made pure with air and with fire...'

He looked across at Flavia.

'...and you would go alone with Malinali. There is a special place, a place sacred to Mayan women that only she knows, a place I do not know myself... And she would make you pure with a ceremony of earth and water...'

An uncertain silence descended on the room. Flavia was wondering what they had got themselves into, wondering whether they had begun to stray into difficult, uncharted waters. She tried desperately to reassure herself. We have come here for a reason, she kept telling herself as she sought the inner strength to challenge her uncertainty. We mustn't back out now, we must trust the moment...

James, too, was working through a similar process. He too had worked hard to counter the fears, and like Flavia he had reached a similar conclusion. Suddenly the tension eased and there was a tangible feeling of trust.

Flavia looked across at James and could sense that he, too, was willing to take the risk. He nodded silently to let her know he was willing to go ahead.

'I think we all agree...' she said finally. 'We feel privileged to share in such a special and significant purpose...to be part of this with you...'

They finished their meal together and agreed to make their preparations the following day. Flavia would meet with Malinali down beside the lake near the dugout canoes. James would meet with Arana down in the town centre near the fountain in front of the church. Then, when they were ready, Arana and Malinali escorted James and Flavia back down to Xocomil, carrying smouldering brushwood torches to light their way along the rocky track.

They all knew that the work itself was just beginning, that important tasks still lay ahead...

25

AT NOON FLAVIA MADE HER WAY down to the foreshore where she had met with Malinali the day before. Then she walked away from the beached dugout canoes in a westerly direction along a narrow stretch of dark pebbly beach. Malinali had told her to watch out for a large boulder that jutted out into the water. After she passed the boulder, she should keep going until she came to a small freshwater creek that opened out into the lake. Then she was to follow the creek inland, away from the lake, up a twisting dirt track which finally opened out into a more level area where there were large patches of thick green grass and small flowering bushes. She would recognise it immediately, said Malinali, because two large ceiba trees were growing there and their small white petals would be scattered on the grass. Malinali would come to the same location by another track and they would then go together to the special women's place, a place where they could be alone by themselves.

As Flavia reached the end of the dirt track she could see the two distinctive ceiba trees reaching high up above the other trees in the canopy. And she needn't have worried about waiting there alone because Malinali had arrived before her. She came over and kissed Flavia on the cheek, and offered her some cornbread and fruit in case she was hungry. Then they set off on another track that would take them higher up the slope... to a special place overlooking the lake.

Silently they scaled the steep rocky track until they came to a ledge where the path headed inland away from the lake. Malinali now called for Flavia to follow her through the dense shrubbery, away from the main track, taking care not to scratch herself on the spiky branches that obstructed their pathway through the bushes.

Soon, however, the ground levelled off again and Flavia could see a clearwater stream trickling into a small mountain pool edged with reeds, patches of grass and clusters of small yellow flowers. On one side was a partially enclosed rock-ledge facing out towards the lake, and just beyond the pool was an irregular fissure in the rock-face which opened out into a small cave.

'This is so beautiful,' said Flavia, 'so exquisitely beautiful...'

The air smelt fresh and pure and a soft clear light was filtering down through the taller trees arching above them. Flavia walked across to the rock-ledge and looked out across the lake. They were really quite high up here. The dense folds of deep green foliage were like a luxurious outstretched cloak sweeping elegantly down to the waters below...

'It's just so perfect...and so still...'

It was true. Flavia was sure there must be scores of bright parrots and other birds high up in the trees, as well as monkeys and other forest creatures, but for the moment there was only silence.

'It's often like this,' said Malinali as she eased her bag carefully down onto the ground. 'It's a special place, a sacred place... You can feel that just by being here...'

She beamed a warm smile at Flavia.

'... and it's also a women's place. Among our people it is only the women who come here... to give offerings and purify themselves.'

She drew forth a long multi-coloured shawl from the bag she had been carrying.

'Zafrina asked me to give this to you as your ritual gift,' she said. 'Take off your other clothes and drape this around you instead...'

When she had done that Malinali asked Flavia to kneel beside her at the entrance to the cave.

'First it is our custom to offer a few drops of blood in service to the Goddess,' said Malinali. 'For our people, blood is the source of life, the life-force of the soul...'

Drawing a small flint blade from her bag she took hold of Flavia's arm. Then she made a small incision, allowing a few drops of thick red blood to ooze down onto the ground.

Then they went inside the cave.

'Wait here at the entrance for a moment,' said Malinali. 'First I must light the candles...'

Reed mats lined the floor of the cave and clusters of large wax candles had been placed around the periphery. Small bowls of coloured earth and pebbles had been placed in the four quarters.

'We honour red in the East, black in the West, white in the North and yellow in the South,' she said. 'These are the sacred colours of the Maya...'

Then she lit each of the candles in turn and burnt some resin in a small earthen bowl which quickly sent exquisite vapours wafting through the cave.

'We do this to honour our Goddess of the Moon and wife of the Heavenly ruler, co-creator of the Earth...'

She looked up at the wall of the cave which until now had been cast in deep shadow.

'There she is,' said Malinali, 'There is our Goddess...'

On the wall of the cave was a painting of a beautiful young woman. She was shown with her distinctive Mayan profile, sitting in a crescent moon, nestling a rabbit in her arms.

'According to the stories we have been told,' said Malinali, 'our Goddess of the Moon was always regarded as a woman of strength and spirit... someone who knew how to express herself and who argued fiercely with her husband, Father Sun, when she felt that it was right to do so. But one day Father Sun became angry with her and cast out one of her eyes. That is why she shines more dimly in the sky...'

She looked across at Flavia, who was listening intently.

'... and that is why she is always shown side-on, in profile, casting her solitary eye down on us. The rabbit she is holding is her companion when the Moon is full...and represents the forces of fertility...'

Flavia smiled to herself. The legends about fertility and the full moon were obviously universal, acknowledged by the Maya as well as by everybody else...

Malinali now knelt in turn towards each of the four corners of the cave, uttering special ritual prayers and placing small gifts of freshly cut corn beside each bowl of coloured earth. In this way, she explained, she was honouring both the Corn Mother and the Moon Goddess. Then she returned to the centre of the cave and began to pray in a soft reflective way, seeking blessings that would flow freely from both Earth and Moon, blessings that would enrich their souls and purify their spirit...

Raising her finger to her lips to request silence she now rose to her feet clutching a small cloth bag and indicated that Flavia should follow her to the clearwater pool.

Slipping off her blouse and unfastening her red *murga* skirt, Malinali eased herself slowly into the rock pool, signalling for Flavia to disrobe and follow her. Then with Flavia in the water beside her she opened her cloth bag, scattering white flower petals across the surface of the pool.

Reaching across and cradling Flavia's head in her arms, Malanali placed a white petal on her forehead.

'We honour the Moon Goddess with petals from the sacred ceiba tree,' she said, beaming down at Flavia, who was now luxuriating in the crystalline waters.

'Close your eyes and open your spirit to the Goddess. Surrender yourself to her... open your soul so her spirit can flow through you...'

Flavia closed her eyes.

'And now, when you are ready, when you feel her spirit has come to dwell inside you, get out of the water and walk over to the rock ledge overlooking the lake. Hold out your open arms and offer your blessing to the Lake Mother, who is the guardian of this place. Speak to her in your own way... with words that come straight from your heart...'

Flavia glided through the clear water to the edge of the rock pool and eased herself onto the grassy bank. Then she walked silently over to the ledge and looked down at the shimmering waters of Lake Atitlán.

She knew then that the lake was a sacred and eternal presence for everyone living around her shores. And she knew also that both the Lake Mother and the Moon Goddess had smiled on them today, that their prayers and offerings had truly been heard. And as Flavia held her arms aloft, she sent her own special song echoing out into the pure mountain air above Lake Atitlán. Out across the shimmering waters of the Lake Mother...

When she had finished Malinali brought over her shawl and draped it around her shoulders. She gave Flavia an enthusiastic hug and kissed her on the cheek. Then they sat down on the ground together so they could dry out in the sun.

'You're my sister now...' she said with a broad smile. '...my sister from across the seas...'

* * *

Meanwhile Arana had arranged to meet James two hours before dusk beside the wall of the family compound. It was only a short distance from Xocomil and James was certain he would be able to retrace the path they had followed the other night. Arana planned to take him to a small cave he had discovered when he had spent those three eventful nights alone on the mountain...where the Lord of the Wind had blown away the demons, where Kinich Ahau had poured the fire of the sun into his chest, and where Ix Chel had transformed herself from a hideous old witch into a beautiful young woman. It was a good place for James to open his heart and spirit, a good place for Grandfather Fire to pour strength into his bones...

Arana greeted James as he arrived and then they went off

together along a steep rocky path that climbed high above the lake. Arana walked on ahead with a large bulging bag slung across his back. James had looked puzzled, wondering what was inside it... Many things, he had told him. Candles, matches, copal incense resin, some small earthenware bowls, a couple of flint knives, two slow burning brushwood torches, a few ritual offerings, two small reed mats and even one or two bananas and avocados — in case they got hungry!

Earlier in the day the lake had been calm and placid but now a gusty wind had arisen and the last of the fishermen were battling with choppy waves as they brought their catch into shore. James could see them down there on the lake, heading for home and then pulling their dugout canoes safely onto the beach.

Arana said they should climb even higher....the cave was just a little further on. Finally they left the track and made their way across a narrow rocky outcrop. Away in the distance, dwarfed by a group of tall pine trees, a small cave was visible, tucked into the folds of the mountain slope.

'I found this place by chance,' said Arana, '... when I was up here on the mountain, not long ago...'

He lowered his bag down onto the ground and took a deep, refreshing breath.

'It was good that I found it. The nights get very cold up here. I was able to gather some sticks and brushwood and light a fire...'

Inside the cave looked dark and a little forbidding. A few discarded clay pots lay scattered around the rough dirt floor and it was clear that incense had been burned here many times before.

'I think a few people have come here to make offerings at different times,' said Arana. 'So we will start from the beginning and purify the place...'

He reached into his bag and brought out some candles and a small incense pot. Then he carried them inside the cave and started arranging them in a circle around the edge.

James watched as Arana lit the candles and then arranged offerings of food and corn in different corners of the cave.

'I've even brought some chocolate,' said Arana, glancing back over his shoulder at his bemused companion. 'Here in Guatemala we make all sorts of offerings to the ancient ones...corn, sugar, liquor, cigarettes and even little pieces of chocolate! In our tradition it is important to feed the gods and keep them happy. Then they will look after us as well...!'

Arana began collecting leaves, twigs and small scraps of kindling so he could start a small fire in the mouth of the cave. After a while, as hot coals and ash began to build up, Arana brought over his incense pot and threw some chunks of brown copal resin into the flames. Then he asked James to take off his shirt and sit cross-legged beside him next to the fire.

As the flames flared up and then gradually died back Arana reached down collecting some warm ash in his fingers. Then he smeared it across James' chest and rubbed it onto his cheeks and forehead.

James flinched as the ash burned into his skin.

'We purify with ash,' said Arana as he rubbed it deeper into the pores. Then he threw some more pieces of solid resin into the fire and blew the billowing incense smoke into James' face and across his chest.

'In this way we honour Grandfather Fire,' said Arana. 'In this way we honour Kukulcan, Lord of the Air....'

He could see that James' close proximity to the hot fuming coals was having its desired effect. Large beads of sweat were now streaming down his chest and moisture was building in his bloodshot eyes.

'Let your sweat and tears drip freely onto the ground,' urged Arana.

'Sweat and tears are like blood... they are part of your life-force, part of your soul...'

He looked deep into James' watery bloodshot eyes to emphasize his point.

'We call this life-force *Itz*. It is part of your power, and it comes from within. *Itz* is like resin from a tree. *Itz* is like milk from a woman's breast. *Itz* is like tears from an eye, like melted wax dripping down the side of a candle. *Itz* is essence... *Itz* is magical power. Our Mayan word for shaman is *Itzam*... Only when you learn to tap your essence – the inner fire that keeps you alive – can you become a true shaman...'

James understood. The heat from the smouldering coals and the wafting waves of incense were burning into his skin but at the same time he felt fresher, stronger... renewed.

Then Arana took out a small flint knife and held James' arm with a firm and steady grip, cutting a small gash in his skin so a few drops of blood fell down into the ash.

'We call the human soul *ch'ulel*. When you offer your blood to the gods you are offering them your soul, offering them your *ch'ulel*... You are building a bridge to the other world...'

He smiled at James to ease away some of the tension that was still there.

'Today I have offered your blood on your behalf. At another time you would make that offering yourself...'

The sun was now setting low across the lake. Arana got up and rubbed his arms vigorously to keep himself warm. Then he bent down beside the smouldering fire, threw in some more incense and walked back into the cave to offer prayers to the ancient ones as a mark of his respect. First he thanked Kinich Ahau, Lord of the Sun, who had bestowed upon his people the priceless gift of fire, a gift for which they would remain eternally grateful. Then he thanked Kekchi, lord of the mountains, who had brought them safely to this cave, high up above the lake. And finally he gave thanks to Kukulcan, Lord of the Wind, who now had a special place in his heart. Then, when everything was done, with the last rays of sunlight retreating from the choppy waters of Lake Atitlán, they got ready to leave.

Slowly they made their way down the mountain, easing their way past the rock ledges and taking care to keep a firm footing on the precipitous path. The dusky haze was now making walking more difficult and they would have to take great care...

But halfway down the mountain Arana felt uneasy, his instincts warning him to beware. Unfamiliar shadows fell menacingly across their track. The wind had suddenly died down and there was now an eerie, ominous silence.

Arana felt someone, or something, was watching them...

They went on a little further.

Now there were stealthy footsteps behind them, surly mutterings that were just faintly audible... distinct and unnerving signs of an invisible, skulking presence...

Arana whirled round to his left. Now he could actually see something...

'Watch out!' he screamed as he sent James hurtling to avoid being hit.

A huge ball of scorching luminous flame flew past them, careening into the shadows.

'It's Ahmok... *Ahmok*...!' yelled Arana. 'He's been watching us, tracking us...'

He looked anxiously down at James, who had scraped his arm against a large rock and was wondering who or what had attacked them.

'It was Ahmok... the dark shaman... my father warned me about him...'

But Ahmok had already screeched past.

The zig-zag line of flame darted ahead and then tapered off in the distance. Soon it had vanished in the darkness.

'He's gone on ahead of us,' said Arana, peering into the haze. 'We must take care with every step...'

Arana reached inside his bag, took out the brushwood torches and lit them with his matches. Then the two men edged their way slowly down the mountain with their torches blazing, taking care at every corner, watching cautiously with every small twist in the track, to ensure that Ahmok did not suddenly leap out and attack them from the shadows.

But Ahmok had disappeared as swiftly as he had come.

Dazed and more than a little shaken, they finally arrived back at the family compound.

'That was a powerful warning...' said Arana, thoroughly relieved they had got back safely.

'It was a warning that we must be ever watchful...a warning that dark forces are always present...'

He put his arm around James to reassure him.

'.... but it is good to know there is strength among friends...'

Finally they walked back down into Xocomil. Arana wanted to be sure that James was safely home at Mama Rosalinda's. This was a day they would remember long into the future... a day when both hope and fear had walked side by side on the mountain... a day when Ahmok had once again made his presence felt.

Flavia was waiting up for him and was delighted when she heard the familiar sound of his voice downstairs, as Rosalinda welcomed him home. She had been reading a book to kill time, hoping he'd get back soon. She had thoroughly enjoyed her time with Malinali and wanted to tell him yet again, even if he was sick and tired of hearing it by now, how great it was that they had made this trip out here to Xocomil. It was indeed a wonderful and truly magical place...

But James looked drained and tired. His face was pale and he looked deeply disturbed. Obviously things had not gone so well for him...

He came over and sat beside her on the bed.

'Arana just dropped me back,' he said, struggling to get his breath back. 'We had a terrifying experience... there's a really dark and threatening side to all this magic...'

Flavia was shocked and surprised. She sat up and put her arm around him to comfort him.

'How do you mean...?'

'There's real evil out there... forces we shouldn't mess with...'

Flavia couldn't understand this at all. This was not the James she knew, the easy-going, down-to-earth journalist with scarcely a care in the world.

'What happened?' she asked nervously. He still looked very shaken up and drained by his experience.

James told her how at first things had gone really well. They had gone to a cave high up on the mountain and there Arana had put him through a purification of fire and air. He couldn't be more specific because Arana had asked him not to share the details. It all happened when they were coming back...

Flavia could feel James' fear returning...

'On the way back we were making our way carefully down the track. It was getting dark. The sun had set and it was getting really hard to see. We were walking back slowly, taking great care, and then suddenly we were attacked...'

'Attacked...?'

'Just out of nowhere... it came out of nowhere...'

'What came out of nowhere...?'

'There was this huge ball of fire... a really huge ball of flame hurtling towards us through the air.... Arana pushed me down onto the ground to get me out of the way and I gashed my arm...'

'And what was it...?' asked Flavia. 'Who was it?' It didn't make any sense...

'We didn't see anyone... it just flew past us and disappeared, way off into the dark...'

Flavia waited for James to continue.

'Arana thinks we were attacked by a dark shaman called Ahmok....a sorcerer who practises evil magic... Arana says Ahmok is opposed to everything he stands for and wants to destroy him...'

Flavia was speechless. Her day with Malinali had been so different...

'This is a lot to take in, last thing at night....'

She squeezed James' arm and kissed him on the cheek.

'Will it be all right if we talk about it later?' she asked, smiling sympathetically. 'Maybe try to get some rest now, and get it out of your mind. Like a bad dream...'

She looked searchingly into his troubled eyes.

He managed half a smile in response and seemed to relax a little more.

Maybe she was right, maybe he should just try to get some sleep...

He shuffled over to the door and Flavia waved him a friendly goodnight to try to lift his spirits.

'At least you got back in one piece and you're safely home. Let's speak about it tomorrow...'

* * *

James was still very quiet and withdrawn at breakfast, haunted by what had happened the day before. Rosalinda brought him a generous omelette with chilli sauce, tomatoes and a few slices of avocado, together with some cornbread on the side.

'Did you rest a little easier?' asked Flavia.

'A little...' he said simply.

He didn't want to speak about it just at the moment.

Flavia felt like persisting.

'Are you sure you just want to bottle it all up?'

James stayed silent for a while but then began to relent just a little.

'Maybe we should go up and see Arana and Malinali, and talk to them about it,' he said. '... ask them what's really going on...'

After breakfast they took the short trek up the hill. They had forgotten to look in the marketplace to see if Zafrina was there but James was sure that Arana, at least, would be home... and maybe Malinali as well.

They came to the low stone wall and went in, following the path through the shrubs and long grass towards the thatched stucco hut. It looked different in the fresh clear light of morning and the view out towards the lake was simply inspirational.

James felt better already.

'Let's go and see if they're there,' said Flavia, making her way past the overhanging palms.

She called out their names and Malinali came quickly to meet them. Arana was there too. Malinali brought them both inside and they went and sat down on the rugs beside the hearth.

'Thank you again for taking me to that special place yesterday,' said Flavia, flashing a warm smile at Malinali. 'But it sounds like Arana and James had a really tough time up there on the mountain....'

Arana shuffled across and sat down beside her. Like James, he too was feeling drained and withdrawn. He hadn't had an easy night and had lain awake through the early hours before dawn, twisting and turning in his hammock just thinking about what had happened.

'Did James tell you about Ahmok?' he asked.

Flavia nodded. Yes, he had told her all about it, or at least the main details about the magical attack...

'Ahmok belongs to a different line of shamans,' said Arana. 'Different from us... opposed to us... He wants to fight everything we do, stamp out everything we hold most sacred...'

Flavia was curious. Why would he want to do that?

'Ahmok's ancestors were aligned with Cortéz, the butcher of our people,' said Arana bluntly. 'The shamans of his lineage still believe in magic but they worship power even more. When the Spanish soldiers overran our people, here in Guatemala, they proved to some that they were more powerful, that they would prevail...'

He paused to drive his point home.

'.. and for Ahmok and his group that proved that the sacred gods and goddesses of the Maya no longer had the magical strength to resist.'

'But how does that affect you?' asked James. He was curious to know how Arana and Malinali fitted in with all this.

'Ahmok knows we are now the custodians of the sacred Calendar Wheel,' said Arana.' He knows that I have been charged with opening the Path of the Sacred Way, and he knows also that we honour the sacred teachings of Kukulcan...'

He clenched his hands and looked down at the floor.

'... Ahmok will do everything in his power to stop us...'

'Do you really believe it was Ahmok who attacked you on the mountain? 'asked Flavia. She didn't for a moment doubt what James had told her but she wanted to hear it directly from Arana himself.

'It was him...' said Arana tersely. 'It was definitely him... He hoped to kill us with his ball of fire...'

'And have you ever seen him in person...actually in the flesh?'

'Once or twice I have seen him here in Xocomil,' said Arana. 'He is a small weasel of a man with a suspicious look and dark untrusting eyes. He lives across the lake, somewhere near Santiago. Sometimes he comes over to the market to sell his wood carvings and make a little money. But most of the people in the market here refuse to trade with him. Some of them say that evil spirits live inside his wooden figurines. They don't want anything to do with him...'

Malinali went away and returned with a plate of sliced fruit for everyone to share.

'As we mentioned the other day, when we first came to Xocomil we spoke with Father Delgado about Kukulcan,' said Flavia, changing the direction of their conversation.'We were interested to find out more about the connection between Kukulcan and Santo Tomás...'

'Well, Ahmok is opposed to everything Santo Tomás stands for,' said Arana. 'Santo Tomás was a man of peace, someone who wished for an end to violence and bloodshed among our people. Ahmok thrives on power, like the conquistadors who came here before him. He will do anything to take control...'

'So what would Ahmok think about Kukulcan?'

'Ahmok would do anything to erase his memory,' said Arana sternly. Arana knew full well that Ahmok would stop at nothing to prevent the coming ceremony from proceeding.

'We had a discussion with Father Delgado about a secret text, the ancient teachings of Kukulcan...' said Flavia. 'He told us there are actual teachings, specific writings, recorded in an ancient scroll. He said he had actually seen them and they have now been translated...'

'It was my brother and I who showed them to him in the first place,' said Arana. 'They were given to me by my father... Fortunately we have got them back again, so they are safely in our hands where Ahmok can't reach them...'

He reached for another slice of fruit.

'The sacred teachings of Kukulcan are now hidden in a cave known only to Malinali and myself...'

Malinali nodded in agreement. She knew that this was true.

'They are in the same secret cave where we will perform the opening of the Sacred Way...'

'So what are the teachings all about?' asked Flavia. 'What did Kukulcan actually say to your people?'

'Kukulcan spoke of another time...' said Arana. 'He spoke of an end to the wickedness and hostility which fills the hearts of people everywhere, in many lands and places....of the anger and aggression that divides families and communities, one against another. And he spoke also of a new beginning... the Second Coming....the beginning of heaven on earth...'

'And did he say when this Second Coming would actually take place?' asked Flavia.

'He told our people it would come to pass at the end of time, when the sacred Calendar Wheel has run its course...'

'And when will that be?'

'At the end of the Festival of Santo Tomás in 2012,' said Arana. '...On 21st December 2012...'

Arana finished eating the fruit and put down his bowl.

'Fortunately the sacred text of Kukulcan is safely in our hands and I truly believe the ancient ones will protect us at all times. Their magic is stronger and more powerful than anything Ahmok could summon up...'

Just at that moment there were heavy splattering sounds on the thatched roof above them. It had started to rain. They all went out to the entrance to look. The rain was thundering down in sheets across the mountain and the lake, the first really heavy rain James and Flavia had seen since arriving in Guatemala.

'That's Chac sending his blessing,' said Arana smiling ironically. 'When the rain god sends a message during the dry season you know it will all end well...'

Part Four

Opening the Sacred Way

26

IT WAS NOW MID-DECEMBER and today low grey clouds had swept in across Lake Atitlán. For once the vast watery expanse looked sombre and uninviting. A cool wind was moving up the mountain and they had quickly moved inside.

Already the conversation had turned to the looming threat of Ahmok and his magical attack on the mountain. For James and Flavia the beautiful landscape around Xocomil and Lake Atitlán had always seemed so welcoming and benign but the encounter with Ahmok had shown them there was a dark underbelly as well...

Flavia wondered whether she should tell Arana and Malinali about her own involvement in the magical arts....tell them about Alpha and Omega and all the work she had done at the castle with her uncle....tell them that she knew about sorcery and the power of evil....tell them she knew how to defend herself against hostile forces. And that just like the shamans here in Guatemala she knew how to call down sacred power for her own magical protection...

She was really uncertain how they would respond. Perhaps it would sound a little presumptuous even to mention something like this. After all, she was a visitor in an exotic country with its own unique magical traditions and Ahmok's attack had been made against James and Arana and not against her.

But Flavia felt relaxed. She was here among friends. Her English reserve had eased noticeably since coming to Guatemala and perhaps there was something she could give back in return.

'There is a technique of magical protection...' she said, venturing suddenly into new uncharted territory. 'Perhaps it is a little out of line even to mention something like this but I was wondering...'

Arana looked surprised. Malinali, too, was caught off guard.

Would they like to see for themselves, she asked finally. She was happy to demonstrate her powers of magical visualisation... they might find it interesting, and maybe even useful as well...

She glanced across at Arana and Malinali. They looked fascinated and intrigued.

What she would share with them would soon become clear. All they had to do, in a few minutes time when she gave a little nod, was just reach in and touch her... just reach across and touch her... that would be the test...

She pointed to her arms and shoulders.

'Push in against me,' she said finally, '...when I give the signal...'

In the meantime they should just sit back silently and observe what was happening...

Arana and Malinali sat down beside her....silent, watchful, wondering what would happen...

For James, too, this had come right out of the blue. Flavia up to her old elusive tricks... Wonderful, mysterious Flavia... who he sometimes felt he knew really well and who at other times seemed just like a stranger...

Meanwhile Flavia had moved into position and was making herself comfortable on a large hand-woven rug. Then she closed her eyes and began to breathe deeply in and out for several minutes before drawing her breathing down to a point where it was almost imperceptible. Soon she had become eerily still, like a frozen statue....her mind and spirit no longer contained by her physical form. It was as if she had entered a completely different space...

It was only faintly visible at first but gradually it became so intense that they could all see it for themselves... Flavia had surrounded herself with a circle of vibrant golden light... an encircling band of pulsing, radiant power. At four points around the circle – to the East, to the West, to the North and to the South – glistening hexagrams were now shimmering in the air around her....charged with magical power and pulsating like flickering tongues of luminescent flame.

Then Flavia nodded her head ... a signal that either Arana or Malinali should try to push forward against the vibrant ring of light.

Arana extended his hand so it gradually encroached on one of the shimmering hexagrams. But at a certain point he could simply push no further. It was like trying to repel a powerful magnetic force, a force much stronger and more resilient than he expected... He tried again, but to no avail...

Then Malinali pushed forward against the ring of light with her outstretched palms. But like Arana, she soon discovered that at a certain point there was no point in persisting. Flavia had literally encased herself within a protective band of pulsing magical energy, creating a barrier as strong and firm as iron.

Then James tried too. He hadn't seen Flavia do this before although he had seen her shapeshift from being a beautiful young woman into a haggard old crone, and that was certainly impressive enough... Flavia's magical powers seemed to know no bounds...

Like the others James found he could push to a certain point, but then no further. There was simply no way to break through the powerful circle of flame...

Then they all withdrew and allowed Flavia to ease back to her normal self. Finally she shook her shoulders, stretched her arms and let out a long yawn. A little while later she took a deep, invigorating breath to signal that her spirit had returned and she had withdrawn her protective magical ring of power.

She had made it all look so easy! Arana and Malinali were greatly impressed. This was really quite remarkable...!

'That really is wonderful magic,' said Arana admiringly. '... strong enough to hold back all sorts of magical attack...'

Like James he was intrigued by the magical powers of this exotic, elusive young woman. He had never for a moment suspected...

'May I ask...?' he began.

Flavia smiled enigmatically, giving nothing away.

'It is indeed powerful magic,' she said finally. 'Sometimes I'm quite amazed myself just how strong and powerful it really is. But just as your gods protect you, the powers I summon are also strong. When I call on them for help they provide powerful and effective protection....'

'Call on them for help...?' Arana and Malinali shrugged their shoulders. What exactly did she mean? They had heard nothing...

'I call inwardly,' said Flavia. 'I summon the force...'

She flashed an ironic smile at Malinali who was still dumbfounded by what she had seen.

'And who knows?' she added cheerily, '... if Ahmok is planning to use his sorcery against us, this sort of magic might come in really handy. We might find it's very useful indeed...'

Later Flavia found herself thinking once again about Lake Atitlán and the adventure that had brought her here in the beginning. There were indeed two faces to this magical place. The Moon Goddess and the Lake Mother would surely guide and protect them but there were other less benign forces out there as well. You could be lulled seductively into the beauty of this place, but there was an edge to the beauty that demanded vigilance and respect. Their eyes had been opened and a lesson had been learned. Ahmok was still out there somewhere and his intentions were clear...

* * *

They walked down into Xocomil together. Flavia wanted to thank Zafrina personally for giving her the beautiful ritual shawl and Malinali knew there would be things to bring back home from the market... fruit, vegetables, a few strands of cloth...

177

anything that remained unsold at the end of the day.

The sun was dipping low in the sky as they strolled across to the square. Zafrina was sitting on her blanket beside the steps and waved as she saw them coming. It had been good today. Most of the corn, squash and beans had been sold but there were still some pumpkins and one or two heavy melons to carry back home.

Malinali was fine with that. She would carry the basket back up the hill and Arana said he would help out as well...

But just at that moment something over in the distance caught his attention. Arana swung round full circle. Now he could see them more clearly. Over at the opposite end of the market two figures were talking in the shadows...

It was his brother Itzamna... and he was here with Ahmok! Ahmok, of all people... he would recognise him anywhere! The two men seemed to be engaged in deep and earnest conversation. Itzamna was gesturing with his hands, emphasizing a particular point. Ahmok, that dark-eyed weasel of a man....! What would he want with Itzamna...?

Arana glanced anxiously at Malinali who was helping her mother gather in all the remaining fruit and vegetables. Then he looked quickly across at James and Flavia who were sifting through some fabrics at a nearby stall. Finally he glanced back towards the corner of the market...

But in the blink of an eye they had both disappeared. Suddenly Ahmok and Itzamna were nowhere to be seen.

'Did you see them?' asked Arana, tugging on Zafrina's shoulder to attract her attention. 'Did you see Itzamna and Ahmok over there...?'

He pointed across into the shadows.

Zafrina shook her head. She hadn't seen Itzamna for weeks, not since he had skulked off to live by himself in the abandoned hut beside the lake. She'd almost given up thinking about him. And as for Ahmok, she didn't even know who he was. She hadn't heard his name before...

Of course, thought Arana to himself. Nachancan had probably kept his thoughts about Ahmok all to himself. In all likelihood there would have been no mention of Ahmok at home, no mention of his evil magic...

But Arana could barely contain his anxiety. He rushed across to the stall where James and Flavia were sorting through a large pile of colourful headscarves.

'I just saw Ahmok ! I just caught sight of him, but then he disappeared... He was talking with my brother...'

They went and sat down together on the old wooden bench in front of the church.

Arana was clearly distressed. He told them about his relationship with his brother so they would understand the situation.

'I can't imagine why Itzamna would want to talk with him...What would they want with each other...?'

James and Flavia could offer little by way of advice. It was indeed a mystery and hopefully they would all find out soon.

Then Malinali and Zafrina walked over. The bags and basket were all packed and ready. It was time to go home, time for them all to walk back up the hill...

For James and Flavia it was just a short stroll back to Mama Rosalinda's. They would see Arana and Malinali soon... maybe tomorrow or the day after that. Obviously there was still much to talk about, much to explore. As they waved goodbye and turned to walk back down to Calle Ramos they could sense that Arana was still very disturbed by Ahmok's presence. It seemed clear that the sorcerer had come here with a purpose. Maybe their encounter with Ahmok was only just beginning...

27

NEXT DAY ARANA CALLED ROUND at Mama Rosalinda's soon after breakfast. He was still worried by Ahmok but there were other things on his mind as well. Pressing matters... urgent things that he needed to tell them and that couldn't be put off any longer...

They walked down beside the lake and sat down on a broad stretch of grass away from the beach. Some of the fishermen were already out on the water. Others were arranging their nets and preparing to sail. Arana wanted to tell them more about his role in opening the Path of the Sacred Way. It was now only a few days away and there were several things he needed to explain...

A gentle breeze was now wafting in across the water. They leaned back in the grass. What was it that he wanted them to know...?

There were several things... he hardly knew where to begin. Firstly, the ceremony would take place at the very end of the Festival of Santo Tomás ... the climax of the Festival...and it would be performed in a cave whose exact whereabouts had to remain secret. James and Flavia were welcome to attend as witnesses if they agreed to be led, blindfold, to the secret location...

Arana explained how the local people depended on their custodians for their very livelihood....that when the Path to the Sacred Way was opened during the ceremony their crops would thrive, the corn harvest would be abundant, and precious rain would fall. And there was another side to all this as well, for when offerings were made and sacred names invoked, the great gods and goddesses would also know that they were loved and respected and then they in turn would send their blessings among the people. So the ancient ones were always there, guarding the ways of the Maya....they were always there guaranteeing food and shelter and watching over the endless cycles of birth, life and death. And it had been this way since the Beginning.

Arana beamed a warm and generous smile at Flavia and James. It was good to be here all together, he told them, good to be here among friends he could trust...He knew this was a lot to absorb but there were so many things they had to know if they were even to begin to understand the ways of his people. And, furthermore, it was a special time now... an auspicious time... There was now a rising sense of hope and anticipation. The sacred Calendar Wheel was edging ever closer, day by day, towards the end of the cycle... towards the time of spiritual transformation... so it was good that James and Flavia had come to Xocomil at this time. It was good that they were here now...

* * *

Early next day James and Flavia arrived at the edge of the family compound where they had agreed to meet. Arana and Malinali were there waiting for them.

They put on the blindfolds and then Arana and Malinali walked slowly beside them along the track, carefully guiding them so they wouldn't slip or fall. Turning in an easterly direction they now walked hesitantly along the path until they came to a dense bush covered with small purple flowers. Then they made their way steadily through an expanse of tall grass and shrubs and up a steep incline towards to a rocky ledge. Here they scaled a large outcrop of basalt rocks and joined another narrow track that led further up the mountain.

Finally they came to a place where two large angular rocks marked the pathway through to a level stretch of ground edged with short tufts of grass. Arana and Malinali guided them through, lowering their heads so they could pass through easily. Then they sensed they were standing on an area of flat paving stones wedged solidly and firmly into the earth. This was surely the entrance to the cave...

Arana went on ahead and Malinali led them both inside. Then she knelt down to help Arana light the large wax candles lining the edge of the cave.

Finally Malinali returned and removed the blindfolds. Flavia and James could see at last!

It was a truly awesome sight. On the floor of the cave large sections of stone had been laid out in the form of a huge sculpted wheel, painstakingly carved with intricate symbols and motifs.

For a moment they just stood there in silence, taking it all in. It was wonderful to be here in this ancient, sacred place. They felt grateful and deeply honoured to be shown something like this...

'When I first came here my father told me something very important,' said Arana. 'He made me realise that these are not just ordinary stone carvings. These stones contain the secret names of our gods and goddesses... these stones contain magical power. This is the Wheel of the Sacred Way. For our people this Calendar Wheel is holy... the very essence of life itself. For us these stones are stones of light...'

He pointed down at the huge stone disc.

'Our sacred Calendar Wheel has two rims, two cycles... This is the ritual Tzolkin wheel that marks what we call the Sacred Round. There are thirteen ritual weeks, each consisting of twenty individual days. They have names like Ahau, Cimi, Caban and Caunac...'

He moved across to another section of the carved stone wheel.

'...and here is the Haab, which contains the eighteen symbols of the sun, each one representing a different month. The Haab moves through a cycle of 360 days followed by five further days known as the Vayeb. Together they make a full and complete year. We call the Haab the Calendar Round...'

James and Flavia were completely lost for words. It was all so ancient and mysterious...

The candlelight was now flickering across the walls of the cave. All around them were wonderful paintings, intricate and accomplished depictions of the Sacred Ones themselves.

They gazed in silence as Arana pointed to each one in turn.

'Here is Kekchi, Lord of the Mountains and Ah Puch, Master of the Underworld...'

He moved round to another section of the cave...

'...Ix Chel, goddess of the Moon and wife of the sun god... Chac, god of rain... Kukulcan, lord of the air... Yumil Kaxob, whose corn sustains us and whose sacred and beautiful flowers inspire us...'

Then he moved across to the other side.

'And here are Itzamna, ruler of the heavens, and Kinich Ahau, lord of the Sun...'

Arana turned and withdrew into the shadows at the back of the cave.

'And here we have something very special... very special indeed...'

He came back holding a roughly-hewn box made of dark, deeply grained wood.

'These are the ancient writings of Kukulcan... the teachings he left here as a gift for our people...'

He pulled back the metal clasp and opened the lid so they could peer inside.

The box contained fragments of an old parchment scroll. It had begun to break into fragments and looked delicate and brittle. Malinali brought one of the candles a little closer so they could glimpse details of the script. The text was completely unfamiliar... strange, angular letters inscribed on the weathered parchment in some form of dye or ancient ink.

'Now you know what has brought you here,' said Arana. 'It is Kukulcan who has drawn us all together... Kukulcan and the sacred Calendar Wheel... and the Final Time itself...'

James and Flavia were deeply awed by the presence of this

sacred, ancient relic.

They looked up at Arana and nodded silently. There could be no doubt about it. This was indeed what had drawn them here... the lure of Kukulcan and the mysterious ancient secret teachings. This was truly why they had come...

28

MALINALI SENSED THAT HER BROTHER was still unnerved by seeing Ahmok down in the marketplace. All morning he had shuffled anxiously around the house, listlessly drifting from one room to the next. Now he was sitting on the floor, hunched up in a corner, lost in his thoughts, a troubled and anxious look written across his face. Yesterday it had been so wonderful up there in the cave. There they had all felt so close, so intimately and personally connected... But on the way back down the mountain she could tell that Arana was becoming tense and uneasy once again... worried about the coming ceremony and the lurking presence of the hostile, unpredictable sorcerer.

This morning she had offered him some fruit but he had just waved it away with a silent sweep of his hand. She had tried talking with him about his concerns... but he had turned and walked angrily away. Now she could stand it no more. She hated seeing Arana bowed down by all these pressures... by all these troubling and disturbing thoughts.

Finally she asked him what she already knew...

'Is it Ahmok who is troubling you...? Is it Ahmok you're worrying about...?'

Arana remained silent, refusing to share his feelings.

She went over and put her arm around him, holding him close.

Couldn't they talk about it now, wouldn't he feel better if he got this off his chest...Wouldn't it be better to share his worries and concerns...?

But Arana was refusing to listen. For the moment he remained sullen and unmoved.

Malinali walked over by the window and looked out towards the lake. She knew the ceremony would have to be conducted the day after tomorrow, the final day of the Festival of Santo Tomás.

That much was certain. Arana would be feeling the weight of all that as well... the awesome, untested responsibility handed down to him by their father. Arana was now custodian of the Path. It had fallen to him, it was his responsibility... She knew it, she understood it, and she felt deeply for him. But they would have to come through all this... they would have to come through it all together.

'Do you want me to go down to the village and find Flavia and James?' she asked. 'If you won't talk to me, do you want to spend some time with them instead...?'

She knew that Arana felt a real ease in the new friendship, a closeness built on trust and mutual understanding.

'Of course it is Ahmok,' said Arana finally. 'Ahmok could still bring us all undone. He has the power, he has great skills in sorcery, and his intentions...'

He stopped suddenly without finishing what he was going to say.

'Who can say what his real intentions are...?'

Malinali nodded sympathetically. It was impossible to tell...

'And what about Itzamna... What would Ahmok want with him...?'

Malinali didn't know. It was all a mystery, all so unexpected...

Then something deeply disturbing flashed through his mind. Something so disturbing that he could hardly bear to contemplate it...

'Are you and I the only ones who know about the cave?' he asked anxiously. 'Are we the only ones who know...?'

But then he remembered they were not the only ones who knew. Itzamna knew as well. Nachancan had taken them there before... they had both gone there together when they were younger... Itzamna knew too... and now Ahmok had returned...

Arana quickly pulled on his shirt and darted past his sister. He just had to get back to the cave to put his mind at ease. Suddenly he felt a lurching, sickening emptiness in the pit of his stomach... It was just too awful to think about...his worst fear...his worst nightmare...

He hurried anxiously along the track, up towards the bend in the path and then as swiftly as possible through the dense grass and shrubs. A sharp thorn had already gashed his leg but still he rushed on towards the rock ledge ahead. Scrambling quickly across the basalt rocks he slipped and scraped his ankle. But there was no time to lose...

Mustering all his reserves he pushed on desperately up the mountain. Then he eased his way through the narrow basalt archway and into the cave itself.

Grappling in the dark, he fumbled anxiously for some matches. Then he lit a candle and moved quickly towards the back of the cave. Struggling to contain his anxiety he reached nervously for the ledge where the box was hidden.

But there was nothing there. The box had been taken...

Arana felt sick....sick to his guts, as if his spirit had been vanquished...

He slumped down onto the floor, his head buried in his hands. It was just too awful...too awful....

After a while he rose sluggishly to his feet. Then he struggled from the cave and shuffled slowly into the daylight.

Now he was blinded by the sun. His eyes were sore, he could hardly see.

He groped his way along the track. Back down the mountain... as carefully as he could.

He still couldn't believe it... now, of all times...

He had to get back to Malinali...tell her what had happened. Together they would have to work out what to do... he could depend on her...

Malinali was waiting for him as he struggled along the path towards the house. Already she knew that something terrible had happened.

'It's gone... it's gone...! Someone has gone into the cave and stolen it...'

Malinali held out her arms and embraced her distraught brother with all the care and support she could muster. She didn't need to ask. He could only be referring to the sacred text of Kukulcan....

It was a crushing and devastating blow... just too terrible to think about...

She paused for a moment as a thought flashed through her mind. There was someone who would know about this... Itzamna would know, he would have to know... Somewhere, somehow, he must have played a part...

Leaving Arana behind at the house, Malinali raced rapidly along the dirt path and down towards Xocomil. Deftly scampering down the track into town, she sped past the markets and on towards the lake.

Just at that moment James and Flavia were returning from a short stroll along the foreshore. They almost collided as Malinali hurtled past.

There was no time to explain.

'Come quickly...!' she yelled as she sped off ahead of them. 'Come quickly....! '

She was blurting out the words as loudly as she could.

'Quickly...Now...!!'

James and Flavia followed rapidly in pursuit. Obviously something really serious had happened. They could find out later what this was all about...

They dashed past the dugout canoes and then out along the sand. Soon they were trudging through dense mud and reeds and splashing their way along the pebbly beach towards Itzamna's hut further round the lake.

Away in the distance Malinali had already scrambled over the beach and was pushing her way through the palm trees. Finally she struggled through the bushes and approached the abandoned hut where Itzamna had taken refuge.

The door was half-open. Inside, on a soiled and dirty mattress, Itzamna lay sleeping, a ragged sheet drawn up over his shoulders. Beside him on the floor was the ancient wooden box.

Malinali darted in, seized the box with both hands and scampered back towards the open door.

Aroused by the scuffle, Itzamna threw off his sheets and reached instinctively for his machete which lay beside him on the floor.

'How could you do this?' screamed Malinali, venting her fury. 'How could you betray us in this way...'

She turned abruptly and ran.

Clutching the box, she pushed angrily through the palm trees, bitterly disappointed by the treachery of her brother. But she hadn't expected to encounter the sorcerer. Some distance away, across the dark volcanic sand, Ahmok was tethering his canoe at the end of the beach. He had come to see Itzamna. Ahmok knew where to find him. They had agreed on a price. Itzamna would simply pass over the box and nothing else would be said...

But when Ahmok saw Malinali emerge from the trees he knew something had happened. Their plan had been disrupted... she was carrying the box ...

He ran swiftly towards her. Whoever she was, she would be no match for him. If he grabbed the box now, the result would still be the same. He would check later with Itzamna and find out what had gone wrong. At least the teachings of Kukulcan would be safely in his hands...

Ahmok darted in front of her, grasping for the box, but Malinali saw him coming and quickly leapt aside.

Then he lunged at her shoulder and tried to force her down. He clutched desperately at her hair and reached out to grab her arm. If he could trip her over and just make her fall...But it was Ahmok who tripped, crashing heavily onto the sand.

He struggled to his feet, thrashing madly at the air. Something unseen was tying him down. Frustrated and angry, he flailed out at his captor. He yelled curses, screamed vengeance...but there was no response. Something, or someone, had tied him to the spot...

Malinali swung round. James and Flavia were running towards her. They had caught up at last...

Flavia looked exultant.

'It worked brilliantly, it was just fantastic...the ring of steel, the ring of power...!'

But now it was Itzamna who was lunging towards them. He looked crazy, distraught... a man possessed.

Swirling round to face him, Flavia steadied her gaze, concentrated her attention and once again brought down the force. Itzamna was trapped. He shuddered to a halt, frozen in his tracks. Now he too was caged in steel...

Flavia signalled towards the canoe. *Quickly...* there was no time to lose...

They ran across the sand and scampered into the canoe. Pushing it clear of the rocks, James grabbed for the oar and began rowing as powerfully as he could, thrusting the blade through the choppy water. Malinali sat towards the front, shielding the box to protect it from the spray.

Soon they were well away from the shore. Then they looked back towards the beach where Itzamna and Ahmok were still caged and trapped by the magic rings of power. They looked pathetic and forlorn... two hopeless men, stranded and alone, their unscrupulous deeds undone....

'It will wear off soon,' said Flavia, amused by their plight. 'The force will wear off in a while, but it worked really well... just when we needed it...'

The canoe cut a straight and steady course through the water. James could tell that Flavia was really enjoying all this... her magic had crossed the boundaries, just like she had said it would. She had made her point, and she had made it with style... just at the right time. For the moment Ahmok had been constrained and it had all worked out well. Now they were heading back home with the force on their side...!

Soon they reached the lake edge at Xocomil. Already the local fishermen had hauled in their dugouts at the end of the day.

'I think Uncle Conrad was watching all this,' said Flavia, as they jumped into the water and dragged the canoe onto the beach. She looked up towards the darkening sky and then out across the lake. 'I think he's out there watching over us, urging us along...'

James shrugged his shoulders. How could she possibly know? It was impossible to tell...

But Flavia seemed convinced.

'I'm absolutely sure,' she said. 'I feel really certain he's been with us all along...'

They walked up the narrow path to Calle Ramos, Malinali nestling the precious box carefully in her arms. She would be all right now, she assured them. She would run back quickly up the hill and then Arana would hide the box somewhere completely safe....somewhere well away from prying eyes and hostile intentions. Today the gods had been kind... their intentions were clear... For the time being, at least, their magic had prevailed.

29

EARLY NEXT MORNING Flavia and James were over in the marketplace talking with Zafrina when a large black car with deep-tinted windows drew up outside the church. Two elegantly dressed men in dark business suits emerged from the car, one with a neatly trimmed black moustache, the other with greying hair and a grim, determined expression on his face. They walked briskly across to the colonnade and then disappeared from view behind the church. Their chauffeur then drove the car over to the other side of the square and parked it a safe distance away from the bustle of the crowd.

James and Flavia were intrigued. They quickly made an excuse to leave Zafrina and darted over towards the colonnade. Peering from the shadows where they couldn't be seen, they looked out across the garden towards Pedro's verandah.

Already the men were engaged in a heated discussion. Pedro was there, and Mario Burri as well. The visitors then sat down around the table as Pedro departed and returned with some drinks. Then they resumed once again, talking in earnest, hunched up together. One of the men then thumped his fist down on the table... it was fascinating to watch.

Flavia glanced back over her shoulder. The driver had unloaded the larger suitcases and was about to bring them across to the church. It was time to slip away so they wouldn't be noticed...

She tugged on James' sleeve and pulled him over towards the bench. Then they sat down and watched as the driver carried the two bulky suitcases in through the garden. Some minutes later he emerged once again, walked back to the car, slammed his door shut, and drove off in a cloud of dust...

It was all so out of character...the unexpected arrival of these sinister dark-suited visitors, their brusque style and manner so completely at odds with the relaxed pace of Xocomil. Clearly they were no friends of Pedro's... but maybe they were colleagues of Mario's. Maybe they had come here on a mission from Rome...?

Later that morning James and Flavia strolled down beside the lake, just to fill in time. Two Mayan women were busy washing clothes at the water's edge. They had hoisted up their skirts so they wouldn't get wet, and some young children were playing on the pebbly beach behind them. Over in the other direction a group of fishermen had brought in their catch and were gutting the fish with sharp short knives, getting them ready to sell at the market.

In a sense it all seemed so familiar... the people, the colours, the textures of the place. The local villagers catching their fish, washing their clothes, caring for their children... everything you would expect in a quiet lakeside community.

But once again Flavia reflected on the dark underbelly around Lake Atitlán. On the one hand there was the Xocomil she knew and loved, but there was also a deepening awareness of those mysterious undercurrents she had felt before. The presence of unseen forces, the sinister unexpected visitors, the skulking presence of Ahmok...

She smiled quietly to herself. At least for the moment she had their measure... together she and Arana would surely ward off any hostile magic their opponents could hurl against them. Already she had a quiet confidence in her skills of magical protection. Now she had put them to the test and they had worked superbly. Uncle Conrad had taught her well, up there at the castle...

They walked back to Mama Rosalinda's and decided to have an early lunch. It was time to unwind, time to chill out. So much had happened... it was good just to take stock for a while and let things be.

But later that afternoon they had two unexpected visitors.

193

Pedro and Mario Burri had come round to see them. They looked anxious and perturbed. There were things they needed to discuss...right now, if they had the time...

They went upstairs and huddled together around the rustic wooden table in Flavia's bedroom. Mario and Pedro sat down on the small wooden chairs and James sidled up next to Flavia on the narrow single bed. Pedro apologized for bursting in like this but there was something urgent that had just arisen...

'We've just had a meeting with two emissaries from Rome,' said Pedro, as he started to explain. 'The Vatican is anxious... Cardinal Ratzinger has made it clear... they want the Santo Tomás scroll to be sent over to Italy. They consider it urgent and want it sent straight away... They want to store it in the archives so it won't fall into the wrong hands...'

He looked anxiously at Flavia...

'We were wondering if you could ask Arana...?'

Flavia understood what he was asking but her suspicions were aroused...

'This is all rather sudden, isn't it?' she asked coolly. 'And why all the urgency...? Why all the concern...?'

Mario Burri looked up from his chair. His expression was sheepish and just a little apologetic.

'I wasn't exactly frank with you when you asked me about the text,' he said hesitantly. 'There are things that I told you that aren't exactly true...'

Flavia remained silent, waiting for him to explain.

'For a start, the scroll doesn't date from the Spanish Conquest... it is actually very old indeed...it is written in the language of Jesus. We think it is the oldest biblical text that has ever been discovered...'

'You told us you had already translated it, that you sent it across to the Vatican...'

'We sent the translation across... but we had to return the actual scroll to Itzamna and he gave it back to his brother. It was part of our agreement...'

'So why all the urgency?' asked Flavia. 'What has changed to make this all so urgent and intense...?'

'It's the script itself,' said Mario, looking down at the floor to avoid her gaze. 'It's the script and what it says...'

Flavia persisted. He would have to be more forthcoming...

'It's about the Second Coming... it changes our perspective...'

An uneasy silence descended on the room.

'It isn't Jesus who is coming, but someone else entirely...'

Pedro could see that Mario was deeply troubled by where this was leading. These were difficult things to express, especially when one had spent an entire career committed to specific interpretations of biblical events...

'The text makes it clear that the Second Coming has nothing to do with the return of Jesus,' said Pedro, responding directly on Mario's behalf.

He paused and glanced fleetingly at his colleague, acknowledging his discomfort.

'It is not Jesus who is coming, but the Goddess Sophia...'

Flavia was lost for words. Sophia! The ancient Goddess of Wisdom! This was a dramatic departure for the Church...

'That's really quite amazing,' she said finally, as it began to sink in.

'It is indeed surprising and also very unexpected,' said Pedro hesitantly.

'...it changes everything we have been brought up to believe...'

Then Mario interjected. Would they at least ask Arana... ask him whether he would hand over the scroll so they could send it to the Vatican?

'We can certainly ask Arana on your behalf,' said Flavia, 'but I'm sure he won't want to part with it. For him the text is like a sacred relic. It is part of his ritual... part of his ceremony. He has told us several times it was a gift to his people... a gift from

Kukulcan...'

Mario seemed unmoved.

'We must obtain the text,' he said tersely. 'We have no other option. The Vatican has told us... the Vatican has commanded...'

'But what if Arana doesn't want to hand it over?' asked Flavia. 'What if he is unwilling to give it to you...?'

'We have been told, quite specifically, that we must retrieve it...'

His eyes had become steely hard.

'We have been told we must get hold of it...*by any means possible*...'

30

THE DAY OF THE CEREMONY HAD ARRIVED. Just after dawn James and Flavia made their way up the rocky track from Xocomil. Once again they had agreed to meet Arana and Malinali beside the wall of the compound. Once again they would wear blindfolds for the journey up the mountain.

Arana had brought with him the box containing the ancient teachings of Kukulcan. Never again would he leave it where someone could come and steal it. The lesson had been well and truly learned, the crisis fortunately averted. His father's words were still loud and clear in his memory: the box should be placed at the very centre of the Wheel. The revered gift from Kukulcan had been gratefully received as a blessing for their people. Through him they had learned to adopt the ways of peace. Through him his people had put aside their rites of blood sacrifice in order to seek a new path in life.

Malinali had brought a large flask of water and the oracle bowl she had been given by Zafrina. Across her back she was carrying a small cloth bag containing white ceiba flowers, freshly gathered blooms that had fallen during the night. These, too, would be offered to the ancient ones in honouring the Wheel.

Soon they reached the basalt ledge and made their way towards the narrow track that led higher up the mountain. Already the early morning sun felt warm on their skin and the air was pure and fresh. Arana felt a strong sense of purpose, a strong sense of duty. It was good to be alive on such a wonderful day!

But as they drew closer to the cave, Arana sensed a lurking, unseen presence. Someone, or something, had gone on ahead. Someone had been tracking them as they moved up the mountain... Someone had been watching them... following their footsteps....

He peered nervously ahead, searching the shadows. There in distance was the tell-tale sign...the darting zig-zag flame they had encountered before. Ahmok had sent his spirit-helper ahead on the mountain...

Arana beckoned silently to Malinali. She had noticed it as well. She reached anxiously across to James and Flavia, drawing them close in beside her on the narrow dirt track.

The flame flared menacingly towards them...jagging through the dirt leaving scorch marks in the earth...

Arana pulled back and wiped the sweat from his brow. Then he heard voices and glanced back down the mountain. Ahmok was weaving his way swiftly towards them. Three unfamiliar, dark-suited figures were scurrying behind, striving desperately to keep up. And further back still, following much more hesitantly, was Itzamna, his treacherous brother... Itzamna, who had betrayed them all...

As Ahmok drew closer Arana moved on towards the flame. He would have to confront it, there was no other choice. He would have to call on his allies...call down his magic....

Steadying his gaze and summoning his strength he called on his guardian to fend back the flame...

Kekchi, Lord of the Sacred Mountains... Kekchi, Lord of the Sacred Temples.... Kekchi, Guardian of the Earth...

The effect was immediate. As the magic words echoed around them, the flame abated and they slipped safely past...

Then he called Nacon, war-god and defender, to bring forth his warrior-spirits. Soon hordes of menacing black shadows were scurrying down the slope....

Ahmok saw them coming and darted to one side. But still they kept coming, swarming over the unsuspecting visitors, obstructing their path and attacking their sweat-drenched skin like hostile mosquitoes.... Mario Burri had already had second thoughts about trekking up the mountain but his colleagues from the Vatican had insisted. Now his worst fears were confirmed. The three men quickly became demented by the swarming spirits. Soon they were twisting and writhing in a state of frenzy, beating them off, scraping them out of their hair. Itzamna had escaped, taking refuge behind some rocks... shielding his face to protect himself from the onslaught...

But for Arana there was no time to lose. As they reached the basalt archway he signalled to Malinali to take James and Flavia quickly inside the cave. Then he turned and waited calmly for the sorcerer to appear...

He had already decided... he must fight evil with evil. He would confront the sorcery, turn it back against itself. Ahmok would soon become his own worst enemy...

As Ahmok lunged into view Arana called Yum Cimil, Master of Destiny... for this god, among all the gods, would expose Ahmok's dark intent...

Yum Cimil, Lord of the Dark Soul...Yum Cimil, Lord of the Dancing Skeletons...Yum Cimil, Dweller on the Threshhold...Yum Cimil, Keeper of the Dark Flame...

The impact was dramatic. For the first time, Ahmok came face to face with his own tormented soul. Rebounding from the force of his own magical power, Ahmok took the full impact and stumbled heavily on the track. Then he rose up again, only to quickly lose his footing on the rubble beside the path. Writhing with pain as he fell against a boulder, Ahmok careened down the mountain slope, his body crashing heavily against the rocks below...

Arana felt exhausted but still his main task lay ahead.

Withdrawing towards the mouth of the cave, Arana steadied himself as he looked up towards the sky. Then, from the very depths of his being he summoned his most powerful guardians – Chiccan, Oc, Men and Ahau: the Four Suns from the Highest

Heavens – and called on them to protect the cave at this special and auspicious time. And as four columns of pale luminescent flame rose up and formed a dome above the cave, only then did Arana feel ready and able to undertake the sacred task that had brought him here. Only then did he feel the power and inner strength of purpose to open the Path of the Sacred Way...

He walked silently into the cave.

Inside, it was a different world...

Already tall white candles had been lit around the edge of the wheel. A soft light was now dancing across the walls of the cave, illuminating the paintings of the ancient ones. Malinali had placed her oracle bowl in the western quarter, the realm of the Lake Mother. Over in the east she had filled another bowl with water, sprinkling it with ceiba petals for the sacred ceremony. James and Flavia were standing respectfully at the edge of the circle... James in the northern quarter and Flavia in the south, their blindfolds removed....

Arana rested the box carefully on the ground and stood in silence at the edge of the great stone circle. He could already feel their sacred presence... the great gods and goddesses who had guided him here today... the great ones without whose care and protection life had no meaning or purpose. Now once again they had come here to support him... to nurture him...to help him move forward. Here in this special place... on this special day of all sacred days... on this special day of Kukulcan...

Then, as the blessings from the ancient ones surged up within his soul, Arana walked over and placed the ancient wooden box at the very centre of the Calendar Wheel. This was its designated place... the very heart of the sacred wheel itself.

First he offered prayers to the four Great Powers...to the awesome and mighty guardians who protected the sacred wheel. Then he reached for his prized stone crystal, the crystal that Nachancan had given him when they had first come here to the mountain. Circling the wheel, he pointed with his crystal towards each stone in turn. And as they resonated in unison, Arana remembered what his father had told him... that the stones in the wheel were alive...that the stones themselves were holy... that their timeless spiritual presence would be renewed as he opened the Sacred Path.

Arana walked over to the eastern quarter, where Malinali had placed a fresh bowl of water on the dark basalt earth. Floating in the water were the white ceiba petals, esteemed by his people as a gift from the gods. Reaching down, he took the bowl reverently in his hands. Then, moving slowly around the Wheel, he placed a single ceiba petal upon each of the sacred sun stones in turn... from Pop and Uo and further round to Pax, Kayab and Cumku. And then, in honouring the Haab, he called each of the sun stones by their own secret names...for these were the names that had been given by Kinich Ahau, Lord of the Sun.

Arana turned next to the sacred Tzolkin wheel, calling all the magical names from Ahau and Imix through to Etznab and Caunac. And when this was done, he could sense already that the Wheel was bursting into life, that the stones of light were moving through their cycles, calling forth the seasons, marking out the days in the great Sacred Round. And he knew then that he had opened the Sacred Way as the gods had decreed. That this was how time had flowed forward since the very Beginning...that these were the cycles governing all Creation...

Already Chac was calling in the rain, already Kinich Ahau was radiating his warmth from the heavens, already Yumil Kaxob was ensuring that fresh new crops would burst forth from the rich fertile soil, already Akhushtal was caring for the spirits of the unborn babies. And guiding all this was the ever-present spirit of Kukulcan... Kukulcan who had brought peace and well-being to his people... Kukulcan, whose message of hope and caring had been with them always.

Now the time had come for Malinali to look forth into the oracle bowl... to seek omens for the years that still lay ahead. For

Malinali knew full well that the Final Time was approaching... that the Calendar Wheel would soon run its course.

In total silence she knelt reverently beside the bowl. Then she prayed to the Lake Mother, goddess of the waters, calling for her guidance... calling for her eyes of spirit to be opened at this special and important time.

Then, when she was ready, she peered into the waters, looking for an omen...

Arana had moved across and was kneeling just behind her. Already so many questions were racing through his mind. Would beloved Kukulcan soon return to his people? Would Kukulcan's teachings of peace endure through all the ages? Would the Final Time be as they had expected...?

Still Malinali remained silent, yielding her soul to the Lake Mother, opening her spirit, calling for an omen...calling for a sign of the times still to come.

Soon images began to flow through the water in the oracle bowl.

Already through the waters of the future, Malinali could sense footsteps approaching ... the footsteps of the Ancient One marking a firm and steady path through the tides of the cosmos... wending their way towards a troubled and war-ravaged world. But even now the face of the Ancient One had not yet been revealed. Even now the name of the Ancient One remained unspoken...

'Is it Kukulcan?' asked Arana anxiously. 'Is it Santo Tomás ?'
She remained silent.
'Is it Jesus...? '
Malanali shook her head...

It was none of these. It was someone whose presence had long been forgotten, someone whose guidance would uplift the hearts of the people, someone whose gifts and special powers would finally transform the world...

She looked again into the waters.

And now she could see indeed that a new spirit was

emerging... a new force for good would soon be with them. That in the troubled and war-ravaged regions of the world power-hungry and misguided men would finally learn to lay down their weapons... that where families had been torn by grief and suffering, instead new feelings of hope and peace would return in their place...

Surely this was the message of Kukulcan, whispered Arana to his sister. Wasn't this what he had taught their people all those many years past?

Indeed it was, Malinali reminded him, but the message in the oracle bowl was clear....

Kukulcan's sacred text had spoken of another teacher... another light of guidance and inspiration....another teacher who would bring healing to the world....

Malanali looked again...

'The Ancient One is a Goddess...' she said finally, as she looked up from the bowl.

'...and her name is Sophia...'

The oracle had spoken...the Lake Mother had shown her...the Lake Mother had made it clear...

'It is Sophia who is coming...' said Malinali, repeating what she had been told. 'It is Sophia who will bring in the New Revelation... I see her footsteps through the heavens...she is approaching even now...'

* * *

Slowly they got ready to leave the cave. Arana felt exhausted and Malinali, too, was puzzled by what she had seen. She knew her brother had expected Kukulcan to return... that this was the teaching they had supported all these years.

But for Flavia it was a confirmation of all that she had hoped for and expected. Pedro and Mario Burri had already told them, and the sacred script of Santo Tomás had confirmed it as well.

The coming of Sophia would see a cleansing of the spirit, the rebirth of Wisdom, the coming of peace and compassion in a completely new form... Human beings were destined to resolve their differences in completely new ways. There had been lessons in all the violence... lessons from the bloodshed... Soon the healing would begin... the healing of the world....

Finally they all walked out into the light. They had all been changed by what had taken place. Arana reassured them...there was no longer any need for James and Flavia to wear the blindfolds if they agreed to keep the location secret. Surely they could trust each other now... they had all been through so much together...

They walked together down the path, heading back to Xocomil. Then, when they were halfway down the mountain, they could see Itzamna waiting for them. He was standing beneath a tree, away in the distance. He was standing there alone, shuffling his feet uneasily in the basalt dust. There was no sign of Mario Burri or the other visitors from Rome.

Arana glanced anxiously at his sister as they walked hesitantly down to meet him. He looked distraught, ashamed...aggrieved by what he had done.

It was a time for healing, a time for reconciliation.

They walked towards him, holding out their hands.

Itzamna ran towards them, tears flooding down his cheeks. He had betrayed their trust, he hoped they would forgive him. Was there an end to all this ... could they all be together once again?

Together they walked back down to the family compound. When they reached the old stone wall Arana and Malinali led Itzamna down the track towards their home. There would be much to share, so much to discuss...

After bidding them farewell James and Flavia continued down into Xocomil. They both knew that their remarkable journey was now coming to an end, that it had all been extraordinary but it would soon be time to return. At least the main work was now done.

31

JAMES WAS SITTING at the large wooden table, finishing his breakfast downstairs at Mama Rosalinda's, when Flavia burst in to greet him with all her news.

She had just phoned home to Uncle Conrad. She had told him it had all been totally amazing but they would be coming home soon...very soon, in fact. And then Uncle Conrad had reminded her they would get home just in time to celebrate Christmas together at the castle and James, of course, was invited as well... Arrangements had also been made for Luis to drive out from Guatemala City to collect them both in Xocomil and take them directly to the airport...at about this time tomorrow....

She paused to catch her breath. 'How about that?' she beamed, leaning across the table with a broad grin on her face. 'It's all arranged...!'

James had never seen her condense so much information into such a short single burst... not even over breakfast. It was a lot to absorb so early in the morning, but he was pleased that she had organised it all... she really was in her element and she seemed to thrive on all the detail...

'And there's something else you might be interested in...'

Flavia smiled provocatively across the table.

'I had a really fascinating dream last night...it seemed to flow on from what Malinali discovered in the oracle bowl...'

She paused for a moment to get his full attention.

'In my dream there was a broad open space like a large square outside an ancient, historical cathedral.... It was somewhere in Europe, somewhere like the Vatican. There were hundreds of women converging on the entrance, praying for peace, praying for wisdom and understanding. I was there... several of my friends were there. Some of the women were wearing long cream robes, lined with deep red silk. They were all filing in, filing into the cathedral by the hundreds...letting it be known that they too had a voice...'

She paused again and then continued.

'And there were quetzal birds... dozens and dozens of them... flying in the air. Twisting and turning... dancing in the air... dancing in celebration...dancing for peace. And then suddenly the doors of the cathedral were flung back and hundreds and hundreds of files and archives came floating out into the air. Floating... just floating... Letting us all know that there were no more secrets...'

'Dreams really are amazing' said James when she had finished. '...they're like a doorway to another world...'

She nodded and smiled. His response was clichéd and predictable but she knew he'd be intrigued...

But the way James saw it, Flavia was even more amazing than her dreams. She really was an extraordinary person... maybe the most fascinating person he had ever met. He hoped, when they got back to England, that they would remain good friends, spend more time together... maybe become even closer...

And yet he had to remind himself, they had come here for a purpose. A professional trip, she had called it. They had to get their priorities right, at least for the time being... and already a procession of characters was streaming through his mind.

Flavia... Arana... Malinali... Zafrina... Pedro Delgado... Mario Burri... Ahmok... Itzamna... Kukulcan... Santo Tomás... and now, of course, Sophia...

The journey had been remarkable and there was so much to tell. They would all be part of his story when he got home to write it.

* * *

POSTSCRIPT

James Highgate's award-winning feature article on Kukulcan
and the ancient biblical text of Santo Tomás was published first
in *The Brighton Herald* – a world scoop for the small regional
newspaper. It was subsequently syndicated to a number of
major international publications including
Le Monde, The Washington Post, Der Spiegel, El Pais and
The Los Angeles Times.

The world now awaits the final revelations of
21 December 2012.

* * *

BOOKS

O is a symbol of the world, of oneness and unity. In different cultures it also means the "eye," symbolizing knowledge and insight. We aim to publish books that are accessible, constructive and that challenge accepted opinion, both that of academia and the "moral majority."

Our books are available in all good English language bookstores worldwide. If you don't see the book on the shelves ask the bookstore to order it for you, quoting the ISBN number and title. Alternatively you can order online (all major online retail sites carry our titles) or contact the distributor in the relevant country, listed on the copyright page.

See our website www.o-books.net for a full list of over 500 titles, growing by 100 a year.

And tune in to myspiritradio.com for our book review radio show, hosted by June-Elleni Laine, where you can listen to the authors discussing their books.

mySpiritRadio